The Craving and the Cross

Herbert Wright

Dedication

The Craving and the Cross is dedicated to human potential,
the purest expression of God's will.

Chapter 1

He awakens, alert and joyful. He smiles and thanks God for his life. It is dark and the streets are barren. He sits up and adjusts his clothing. He places his forehead on his folded hands and he prays. He will remain this way for several minutes humbly giving himself to the will of the father. He then sits erect, but not stiff, his eyes are closed and he breathes deeply. He lets the divine energy inhabit every cell in his body.

He completes his prayers and clears the debris from around him, he is careful not to wake his neighbors. He ignores the foul odors of old wine and fresh urine. He watches rats dart in and out of garbage cans and cracks in the wall. He hears echoes of the boisterous voices as teens pass by the alley. Gradually the echoes fade and he is again in touch with his inner voice.

His shoes have been taken so many times so he no longer wears them. He has let his hair grow long and he dresses simply. His body and tattered clothes are always clean. His eyes and teeth are white. His wiry body is strong and he stands erect. Energy oozes from his eyes.

He heads for the bathroom outside of an Amoco station. He lingers outside and waits for an opportunity to enter. He washes every inch of his body. He revels in the joy of cleaning. He can feel his pores breathing. He feels renewed. He finds a bench and indulges in his favorite past time, observing people.

As he sits and watches, a man stops abruptly because a dog has crouched and defecated in his path. The man has a look of surprise and disgust. It is a look familiar to the homeless. He has seen it often from people startled by beggars.

He knows these men and women do not think of beggars as people. The homeless are simply the dirt they see and the odors they smell. Beggars are little more than offenses to their senses. They are a disruption to the pleasantness of the day and a reminder of the fragile security of their own lives.

He looks and he waits. He knows that God will give him a task today, so he looks for an external sign. This is hard for him, he prefers God to appear within him. He loves hearing that voice that makes him feel like he is surging with power and gentle like a lamb. When God calls him to major tasks, he first hears demons, then angels. They fight against each other until he feels his head will burst. He sweats, he shakes, and then the almighty tells him what he must do.

Most of his assignments are not major tasks. They are simple. He knows that the little things matter too. He remembers the Butterfly Effect. He remembers a butterfly flapping its wings somewhere can cause a hurricane hundreds of miles away. So it makes sense to him that his daily kind deed can have wonderful repercussions for humanity.

Two men approach him. He has seen them before. One man has on two coats that are different sizes. One coat is too long and the other too short. The long coat is plaid and the inner coat once white is now gray from dirt. He remembers that the man's name is Wally. He has a far off look in his eyes. Wally glances at him for a second to size him up before sitting. When Wally sits, Wally pushes him slightly to establish dominance. He ignores the push.

The second man is wearing a wide blue striped tie, a tweed jacket and a long wool coat. His jacket and tie have layers of dirt but it is apparent that the man is still looking for work .They sit on opposite sides of him.

Wally, the man with the two coats immediately starts listening to a voice in his head compelling him to alternately shout and whisper as people pass by. Ben, the man on the right speaks to him.

"Hey Joe, how are you doing?"

"Bless you, my friend. I am fine. Thank you for asking." He answers.

"Have you found anything to eat today?" Ben asks.

"I have a partially eaten apple, would you like it?"

Ben takes it quickly. As he eats, he asks, "What are you going to eat?"

"The Lord will provide." Joe answers.

Ben quickly angers, "The Lord? Provide what? He ain't providing shit for me or you either. I lost my home, my savings, and my damn job."

Ben gets up, starts to pace, and kicks at the air. Joe looks at Ben while remaining on the bench.

"My daughter said 'Daddy please, I need food, I'm hungry' and I could hear the sounds of hunger rumbling in her belly, I saw desperation in her tiny eyes. I begged God to help. He did nothing."

Ben's voice cracks as tears begin.

"I have never felt worse in my life. I could not keep my child from starving. She was trembling from the freezing cold. Where was he? When my wife took them to her parent's house, I felt relieved. Now I feel dead inside. Nothing, not living on the street or being kicked and stabbed for my coat, nothing is even close." Joe watches Ben, his eyes fill with tears as he feels Ben's pain.

Joe says, "I have an orange too, would you like it?"

Ben sits back down. He takes the orange.

"Did you hear what I said?"

Before he could answer, Wally yells, "The TV antenna is in my spine." He scratches his back until he hits the right spot. Wally smiles, drool escaping from his lips, he looks toward them.

Wally sees Ben eating and snatches the bag, he looks through it frantically and finding nothing, he tosses it to the ground. Joe looks at Wally and then turns back to Ben.

"I will pray for you, Ben .What would you like God to do for you?"

"Make me as I was before 2004. Give me back all I lost." Ben said sarcastically while sort of wishing that it could somehow magically come true.

"So you want to be the man you were before?"

"Exactly." Ben says.

"Would you have given food to any of us or even looked at us as you passed by? Did you hear the plea of any of the world's hungry?"

Ben replied furiously, "Who the fuck do you think you are. Are you perfect? Oh that's right you demented bastard you think you are Jesus. Isn't that right? They call you Saint Bum, His Homelessness, SOG, the Son of Garbage. Ain't that what they call you?" Joe does not answer.

"I'M INVISIBLE, YOU CAN'T FIND ME." Wally chimes in. He makes obscene gestures at pedestrians and laughs, confident that he is unseen. They both ignore Wally.

Ben continues. "You really need to make that appointment. Get some help. You have the nerve to give me advice. Who are you anyway?"

"I am you."

"You are me?" Ben replies, "I am not a sick fuck pal. You are more like Wally over there than you are like me."

A policeman approaches and hits the bench hard with his nightstick

"Get moving", he says and they all move in different directions. Joe walks and waits for a sign. He walks all morning, he smiles at everyone who will make eye contact with him, there are few. At lunchtime, he arrives downtown.

He will eat what others throw away. He has a strategy. He will only eat the discarded food of people he senses are good. His eyes will also follow thin people since they are the most likely to throw food away.

He likes fruit, nuts and fish. The only fish he gets to eat is tuna. He collects all he feels is edible and heads for Central Park.

It has been an uncharacteristically warm winter in New York. He enters Central Park at 57th street and walks through the park to a small hill where he can watch children in the playground. He feels this is a place of sheer joy and life in the moment. The children overcome fear on the monkey bars, feel heights of exhilaration on the swing, learn cooperation and shared reward on the seesaw. The children are running. There is laughter and a gleeful chorus of energy that is duplicated by few things in human experience.

Their energy fills him. He wishes the greatest of all possible destinies to each child. He then looks beyond them to the cold gray buildings that dwarf everything around them. He wonders how many of their innocent, joyful lives will be effected by the decisions made in towers like these.

"Hey you pervert, what are you doing watching the kids?"

"What?" Joe says.

"You heard me, are you planning to snatch some kid?"

"Where would I take a child, I have no home or no car to put him in." Joe says. The man is confused for a moment and does not respond.

He then says, "You better get out of here."

"I love it here why would I leave?" Joe says.

The man takes out his cell phone. "Do you want me to call the cops?"

"No." Joe says. He loves this spot but the man will probably not be back tomorrow, it is easier just to leave.

"Were you sent by the men in the big buildings?" he asks.

The man just stares at him and points for him to go. When he reaches the street, he is arrested based on the description that the man gave of him. Police handcuff him and take him to the precinct.

When he arrives at the station, he takes a seat next to two men who glance at him when he sits, they determine that he is harmless and continue with their conversation as if he is not there.

"So the bitch leaves me cause I hit her. I was ready to fire her anyway so I let the bitch leave. It's not like that shit was new to her, her step-dad used to beat her ass. That mother-fucker was a piece of work! He used to tie her mother's hands on that pole that goes across the top of the closet."

The second man says laughing, "You mean he used to hang that bitch up like a coat?"

"Yeah, then he would undo a hanger and bend it until it was straight and whip her with it. Then his ass would go watch tv or something and just leave the bitch hanging there for hours."

"For hours?" says the second man astonished.

"Yeah and it would be over some stupid shit like she wore red on Tuesday or she served him a food that had an r in it like fucking rutabaga." They laugh.

"I remember when I first started dating the bitch and I would pick her up. Her Mom would be in the closet and I was like, do you want me to call somebody, get help, some shit you know. She was like uh, no it's all right, let's just go. You know later, after I got to know them better, she would be in the closet and say 'Hi how you been.' You know have a fucking conversation from the closet like that shit was normal." The second man is laughing

The first man continues. "Yo and check this out, her little brother is watching TV with the father and goes to the refrigerator and yells Mom we're out of fruit loops, like he expects her to get them and shit. And that bitch want to get mad at me, she should be happy all I did was smack her ass."

Second man asks, "So where is she at?"

"Peep this, she goes down south to find her real dad, he lives in Westbumfuck, Alabama or some shit. He hasn't seen her in 15 years. He says he is sorry he left her, he is going to kill the stepfather, blase this blase that. She calls me tells me how I'm a piece of shit and how her life is going to be so much better. Then the father gets high, asks for a hug and tries to fuck her. So she comes crying back to me and I mean this bitch look like she just escaped from a mental hospital, I mean like that look you see in the movies when the killers coming. That's how she looks all the time now."

The second man says, "I thought she called the cops on you, why you here man?"

"That motherfucker messed up my girl. I drove down south and maimed his ass. They found me so I have face charges in Alabama. Nobody messes with my baby; you know what I mean slick." The second man nods.

"And dig, I got this connect downtown. This high-powered dude I do some work for some time, he really has juice and I hope he can get me out of this shit."

The second man says, "He got it like that B."

"Yeah, just like that. He owns a whole fucking skyscraper uptown. This dude got worldwide shit."

Joe is sitting quietly, ignoring the men, when suddenly he feels the demons. He can smell them. He tastes their bile on his tongue. He feels nauseated, like he is about to throw up but instead the demons expel their voices into his head. Their words demand his death, by command, by urging, by using the voice of departed loved ones and one loud persistent voice, his own. He feels intense revulsion and fear. He is desperate and anxiety overwhelms him.

If he had an ax, he would cut off his head. When the pain reaches the pinnacle of his tolerance, he sees the angel. She flies toward him, rays of light emanating from her fingers. She enters through his eyes. The light temporarily blinds him and the voices still cripple him. Outwardly, he is immobilized. Inside the battle has begun. He feels them all over his body, they crawl up his legs, and they wrestle in his heart and descend into his liver. The war advances and each conquer one side of him. They vie for his mind, soul and his body. He feels like he is chained to two horses about to race in opposite directions and rip him apart. Then he hears the one voice. Everything changes instantly. He feels sheer joy so intense it is tangible. His body tingles with energy; his mind vibrates with enlightenment. His hand touches the garment of infinity.

The Great Voice says, "My son, your duty is clear. You must go to the cave of the vampire and bring light. The bleeding must stop." With that, the great voice and all that preceded it leave his body.

"Hey are you ok?" "What are you on?" The cop shakes him.

He tries to compose himself.

"Come with me." the policeman said. Joe's mind is elsewhere, he tries desperately to let the presence of the Great Voice linger and to remember his message exactly.

The cop repeats himself, "I said get the hell up."

The two men sitting beside him are laughing at him. They have watched him the whole time. They saw him talk to himself, scream in pain, stiffen like a board and now he has this fixed goofy smile on his face.

One man said, "Man that must be some new shit you're smoking."

The second man said "No that must be those legal drugs they advertise on TV. You know, may cause this, and may cause that. You should have read the fine print, homey."

He walks away with the police officer who tells him to have a seat.

"Name?" Joe is quiet. "Hey didn't you hear me. What's your name?"

His nerves are still tingling from his powerful experience, his body occasionally shakes, an after-shock of delight. He is oblivious to the policeman's question.

"Hey", the cop yells, "Are you deaf?"

Reality is vague; his vision is hazy.

"What?" he says.

"Listen you freak, you got one more time to answer my question. I hear- I don't know, Hari Krishna or any other bullshit and you are going under the jail."

He hears every other word like his brain is a cell phone that is out of range. He can feel the policeman's anger, so he responds.

"Sir ask me anything you like I will be glad to cooperate."

The cop says, "Gooney bastard, what's your fucking name?"

"I am the servant of He who is great. You may call me what you wish."

He sees the cop's eyes redden and the veins in his temple bulge, so he quickly adds, "I was kicked in the head many times by a group of misguided youth. I don't remember my name and anticipating your next question, I live on the street, and most people call me Joe, sir."

The policeman calms down. "I gotta put something down, you want John Doe?"

He waits for inspiration, finding none, he says "How about Joe C. Doe?"

The policeman answers, "I don't give a fuck."

He likes the name and decides he will use it from now on. Occasions where he has to use his full name are rare. Yes, this suits him he thinks. He is finishing the booking process .The policeman gives Joe a Desk Appearance Ticket but he does not leave. He feels he must talk to one of the men who sat next to him before he heard the great voice. He senses that he is the key to his great mission. He looks everywhere but they are gone.

Chapter 2

It is the dawn of a dark, rainy day. The clouds spew smog-tainted teardrops from a dismal sky. Haze and fog distort the view of the rising sun. Its' beauty and power are overwhelmed by the dreary, insistent plodding of darkness. Lightening darts out, briefly illuminating the sky. It is captured by the lighting rod on the tall, gray skyscraper where the minions of the Reversal' Corp. are hard at work.

Cleo F. Bloodworthy is the CEO of Reversal' (pronounced ree-ver-SAL') and he has already left the building. He prefers to work at night and leave before dawn. His executives think he is an eccentric genius and they don't care when he comes to work as long as he keeps making them filthy rich.

He is on their I-pods, he teleconferences, he texts, he twitters but he doesn't do lunch. Reversal' is the sixth largest corporation in America and is a world leader in bio-foods, defense and media.

Food was his first business. He worked at the Kill-floor at a company that sold pork to supermarkets. He and his coworkers slaughtered pigs. They used saws to dismember the pig's bodies. While life was fading from the pigs, pieces of blood and flesh splashed against his goggles and his face. He wiped it from his brow and occasionally it dripped into his mouth.

Later when he owned the company, he would still return to the Kill-floor at night and slaughter pigs. His employees admired him for this and thought he was one of them. He just enjoyed the work .He had come to accept that he liked the feeling of power he felt in killing and quartering pigs. However, it was more than that.

He liked the kill floor the way a basketball player in a gym likes the echo of the ball as it hit the hardwood floor or the squeak of his sneakers when he pivots. He liked hearing the pig's squeal, the crack of the bones and seeing the blood pouring into floor drains from all directions.

He would eventually open new businesses all over the world. He was happy with his success and had killed pigs in Brazil, Mexico, Canada and Italy. He took vacations only in places where he owned businesses. Part of the vacation always included killing pigs.

He was not then a public figure. Yet he was already associated with beautiful and successful women. These women of beauty often had kinky affectations. He could sense it. He had no doubt or fear and would always approach women confidently.

He was barely six feet, stocky and with a boyish appearance. He had a full head of hair slicked down like from a bygone era. He dressed immaculately but when he took off his jacket, you could see the hair on his back. He always spoke with his hands locked behind him. When he looked at you, you did not know if he was excited or crazed.

Often he took his companions home. There they were drugged and awakened in the master bedroom of one of his palatial homes. They found themselves draped in satin sheets, tied with heavy twine and covered with pig blood. He was an insatiable lover, lusting as much for the blood as for their bodies. Slurping, licking, writhing, probing, his passion became theirs and most of these women left startled and still tingling. When women made a fuss, he paid them for their silence or they mysteriously disappeared.

It was while he was dismembering a former lover at his Kill-floor in Brazil that he discovered that human and pig blood made a nice cocktail. It was to be his beverage of choice for all his sexual encounters.

Although he was consumed by lust, he was always the consummate businessman. So when he was approached by one of his executives about bio-foods, he listened. The executive explained that this was an emerging high tech industry. He explained how seeds could be developed that were drought resistant and other seeds could be created to make a smell that repelled predators. Once we owned this science, he explained, the company could make a fortune.

Cleo Bloodworthy knew at once that this was a great idea. He read the research that was available at the time and bought a small company called Genuflect, which had the best ideas and most promise.

The President of Genuflect was a scientist not a businessman. He tried to hold on to the company but Cleo convinced his colleagues that they would never be able to do their important work without constant worry about funding. Cleo convinced them that if they joined him, they would never have to worry about money again.

He presented an immaculate business plan and showed a sincere interest in their product. They all recoiled at being owned by a Pork company but eventually were overwhelmed by the logic of the deal.

The business became tremendously successful except for a few places in Europe where foods are labeled as bio-engineered. In the U.S. the agri-businesses embraced the new seeds because they minimized financial loses. It was just another advantage for the mega-farmer.

Smaller farmers bought the seeds in order to compete. In ten years, 70% of grains, oats, bran, corn and wheat in the U.S. came from bio-engineered seeds and Cleo owned 80% of the industry.

He always disliked the President of Genuflect. He was so weak that Cleo had to spend huge amounts of time running the company, which kept him away from the pork business. On the sixth anniversary as CEO of Genuflect Cleo Bloodworthy invited the ex-president of the company, Skip Holden, over for drinks. He was a small, thin man who never looked anyone in the eye except when he was talking about science.

Cleo, had in two years, changed Skip Holden from a leader to a cowering jittery pawn. Bloodworthy killed Holden. Holden's blood was later poured from a finely cut glass over the breast and belly of a tall Italian model.

"How does it taste?' She asked.

"A little weak, my dear, it lacks character." He said.

Cleo began his media business as a response to organizations that picketed his first business, Prime Pork. They said the way he killed his animals was especially cruel. He started a regular column in the Penny-saver and anonymously wrote letters to the editor of the town newspaper calling the protester's organization a "Radical hate group infringing on the freedom of legitimate businessmen."

That same newspaper began to have problems with vandalism. Windows were broken, offices trashed. Police blamed the protesters although they never proved anything. Cleo said the vandalism was a result of the paper's printing letters in support of his business.

He told the newspaper he wanted to help and asked to become a member of their board. Once he saw their books. He started pushing for a more sensational style of journalism, one of advocacy for decent values and a strong community.

He hired a new editorial staff, seduced powerful new advertisers and hired an in-house PR team to promote his ideas. His value-laden, low-cost, fear-provoking style became an instant success. He had no journalist, just commentators revving up the emotions of the readers.

He used this same model to take over newspapers all over the country. He bought radio stations in small markets. He syndicated his very popular commentators to small budget radio stations at no cost but required the radio stations to give him all the national advertising slots available during the time the commentators were broadcasting. This replicated the number of stations and the profit nationwide. Media became his most successful business and caused the slow, lingering death of real journalism, which was no longer cost effective.

He became a player in the defense industry almost by accident. When he took over Genuflect, he noticed that the Defense Dept. had made inquiries to the company about bio- technology. They wanted to use it for national defense.

Skip Holden had refused to have anything to do with weapons but as the company expanded, Cleo saw opportunities where Skip had seen peril. At the top levels of the Defense Dept. and CIA, he participated in discussions of how the government might implant in seeds slow acting poisons, dopamine enhancers, immune –system weakeners and at his suggestion, cognitive debilitates, since an ignorant population is excellent for business.

When some at the CIA balked at his ideas, he reminded them that an ignorant population is also easily controlled. He did not get the contract.

He did make contacts, however, which led to a contract for research in chemical and biological weapons of a more conventional type. Once in the world of government contracts and acquisitions, he created better, streamlined budgets and dependable products. He gained a solid reputation with the Government Accounting Office and a few choice Congressmen and Senators.

Cleo Bloodworthy is now age 50. He is a very accomplished man for his age. He is a regular guest on business news shows on his network and others. Because of his talent for attracting beautiful women, photographers pursue him and his pictures are occasionally inside the pages of People and US magazine.

"I am my own hero." Cleo thinks as his executive staff leaves the meeting room of his home. He had met with the chief of operations for each of his primary businesses as well as the miscellaneous businesses, which included his pork products.

These men were smart and tough enough to run his businesses but weak enough to fear him. They have qualities; he has character. The only men he feared were the men who ran the dark side of his operations. The mercenaries that strong-armed union officials of his media company, the mob guys he laundered drug money for and most feared of all the middle-eastern and African traders who he sold weapons to at an incredible profit.

He closed the door as the last executive left. Now that he had concluded business, he could let his mind fully immerse itself in erotic thoughts of her unending beauty. Her name is Tiffany Mercedes

Rockwood. As she enters; his eyes soak in every inch of her. It is love at first sight every time he sees her. All other women had quickly lost their magic after he possessed them. His lovemaking required such servility that he never again saw them as the objects of beauty or purity he imagined. They were the shell of a fine lobster on a dirty plate. It was different with Tiffany; he always wanted more of her.

He wondered, was it her smell, some subtle curve, her accent, or her smile? He thought about it many times in the two years since they first met. He finally concluded that it was her ability to make love so frenetically, while being dispassionate. She made love to him with energy, skill and imagination but something was missing. It was not the detachment of a prostitute, he was sure she was into him. He could make her come hard; he could not make her eyes sparkle.

In his attempt to make her completely passionate, completely his, he treated her better than he treated anyone else in his life and he was excited about the challenge.

She walks in wearing Victoria Secret under a sexy suit with a short skirt. She crosses her long, taut, curved legs. The light fabric caresses her flawless skin, inching ever so slightly up her thigh. It creates a flimsy, seductive barrier, like tissue paper over exotic chocolate. She fondles the stem of her glass playfully, kicks off her shoe and points her toe. She focuses her doe-like eyes upon him and gives him a wry smile.

He comes toward her and before he can sit, she stands quickly and places her back to him. She grabs his tie and leads him to their special room.

Once there, she whispers, "Close your eyes."

She leaves him standing there while she goes to her car. She returns minutes later with her bag. While his eyes remain closed, she removes two quarts of pig's blood in a distinctive wine bottle, different size paint- brushes and long scented candles. As he is lying on his stomach, she uses wet and dry brushes to paint, tickle and titillate. She paints his inner thigh with a small brush using a gentle touch. She paints the back of his sack and then inserts an inch of the brush into his anus. He turns to resist and she places the burning candle in his hand and forces him to pour the hot wax on her for her bad deed.

He gets the game. He slaps her and takes the brushes. He rips her jacket open and the buttons fall silently on the rich carpet. He throws her on the bed and she lies face down. He uses the wide brush to paint her spine, the back of her legs. He uses the brushes to probe. When he goes too far she burns him with candle wax. They continue for hours in this way until they are covered in blood and wax and asleep in each other's arms.

CHAPTER 3

Wolf is Bloodworthy's television Network. Wolf's news anchor is a huge fat man with a crew cut. The anchor has a large audience of religious and conservative listeners. His devotees admire his leadership. In fact, when listeners call in to his radio show he greets them by saying 'Wolf News' and they respond 'For the Sheep.' They even refer to themselves as Mutton-heads.

The interviewer, although interviewing his boss, is not nervous. He knows that Cleo Bloodworthy would never invite him to his home for dinner. Yet, he also knows that he is a huge moneymaker for Wolf. Bloodworthy would fire him in a minute for bad ratings but never on a whim. Although he had met him three times before, once at his final job interview, once at one of the rare meetings that included people on his level, and once at a cocktail party, he introduces himself as if meeting him for the first time.

"Hello Mr. Bloodworthy, Beck Lowbrow, glad you could make it sir."

"It's a pleasure Beck, glad I hired you, you're doing a great job."

"Those huge paychecks are a great reminder of that sir." Beck responds.

"Where do you want me?" Cleo asks.

"Sit right here please."

Cleo says, "Beck I need you to endear me to your audience with some values stuff and then I want you to help me with the defense budget. I have quite a few contracts that might be in jeopardy if these cuts are allowed."

"No problem, Mr. Bloodworthy, anything else?"

"How long do we have?" Cleo asks.

"Twelve minutes interrupted by two commercials. The first segment values, second segment defense. Ok, we have two minutes to air."

"Sounds good." Cleo says.

They sit with Beck babbling and Cleo looking at his papers until Bloodworthy gives him a look that Beck rightly interprets as shut up. The on air light flashes and Lowbrow begins.

"Citizens, keepers of American freedom, I have a very special guest who is going to give you the lowdown on the socialist, the givers of your hard earned tax dollars to lazy, government leaches. These giver-lovers don't care for you, they won't help you but they love the leaches. Well now they want to take away more than your taxes, they are risking more than our economy, they are jeopardizing the lives of your babies as they sleep in their crib.

"How do I know? I can tell you that because of today's guest. He is a captain of industry and of virtue. He knows how to create jobs and keep America strong. No, I am not talking about some shady politician.

"This is a man that his built three thriving businesses from the ground up. He has a clean mind and dirt under his fingernails. He is

Cleo Bloodworthy, the father of Wolf News and the reason that we have good, honest news, an alternative to liberal mind control. Citizens I have the honor to present to you Cleo Bloodworthy. How are you today, Cleo."

"Blessed by my lord and savior and living the American dream."

"Wonderful. I don't know if many in our audience are aware that you were Forbes man of the Year and the Assemblies of Moral Values Protestants Man of the Year."

"Yes that's right Beck." Cleo says. "I also read where you donated uniforms to start youth baseball teams for the children of our troops fighting for our beloved nation."

Cleo responds, "Yes, well I think everyone should do their part."

"You make me proud to be an American!" Lowbrow adds.

"Now let me ask you just a few questions because you hear so much from liberals. Let me just get your opinion on just a few issues in the news today."

"Sure." Cleo responds.

"Let's start with abortion, the killing of babies by all these loose liberal whores that claim it's their body, but they give it to any Tom, Dick and Harry who asks."

Cleo responds, "I don't like to judge other people but it is hard not to. Everyone has sexual urges and they can be powerful. Yet good women have strong morals, good families and the church to guide them through these times of difficulty. Liberals reject the church and family and their only commitment is to their own pleasure. That's why you find so many of them use drugs and kill the unborn."

"Great answer, are you listening out there? What about Gay marriage?"

"You know the answer to that one, Beck. Sex is between a man a woman and I think best in the missionary position only. I know that sounds a little old-fashioned but I really believe it. I think once you start trying all these different positions, you start thinking like a beast. I think sex with a man is complete capitulation to the devil. We must keep our mind clean and pure so that we can be a vessel for the almighty not a toilet for our lover's lust."

"Final question before we have to take a break. What can we do to save America's declining morality? Before you answer, I am not saying America is declining. We are the greatest country in the world. I mean what can loyal Americans do to keep the haters of America, foreign and domestic, from changing the character of the country we love?"

"I think we must realize that we are in a life and death struggle for the minds of the American people. They try to tell us that things we know to be true are false and act as if we are morons if we believe our own minds. Gay sex is wrong, illegal immigrants take our jobs and taxes, Muslims want to kill us, Blacks use Affirmative Action to take jobs from whites that are more qualified, unions cost us jobs and tax cuts keep our money in our pockets. America fights for freedom.

"Don't think about what I have just said, that's what they want you to do, just feel. Doesn't all that just feel right? Thinking is a way for all those guys with PHD's to brainwash you with their socialist propaganda. Doesn't that just feel right? I mean in your gut. Yeah, believe yourself; honor your own feelings. That's what I would tell our patriots."

They go to commercial.

"Wow, what a great job, sir. You should have your own show!"

Cleo winks, "I do." He smirks and goes back to his notes.

The light blinks, indicating it is time for the second segment.

"Ok. Didn't I tell you? I know you all wish you had a leader like this at the helm of your company. I know some of you have to work for liberal trash. You have no choice and we understand you, we do. You cannot choose who you work for, you have to find work wherever you can. But, if you could choose, wouldn't you want a god-fearing, patriotic father figure as your boss. Cleo let me ask you just one more question. Our Pretender- in Chief wants to reduce the budget to protect America.

"He wants to place us at the mercy of terrorist, pirates and nuclear threats. He thinks he can make us better by making us weaker. By making us weaker, he is actually conspiring with those who want kill us. Doesn't that make him a traitor?"

"I don't think the President is a traitor but I do think this. If you chose a mechanic to fix your car and he accidentally, with the best of intentions, cuts the brake you still end up dead. The defense of this nation is the primary responsibility of government; it is its most important task. Cut everything before you cut defense.

"It is like your city or town. You make sure police and fire fighters budget is in place before you spend money on the Save the Three

Feathered Nutbird Festival. The federal government does not seem to have its' priorities in order. It wants all these spending items and a strong defense too.

"You can't have both. It's more than wanting to have their cake and eat it too. They don't want to buy milk and eggs and butter and want to eat cake."

Beck Lowbrow, genuinely impressed with his boss' performance, fawns and flatters, Cleo simply nodded and left.

Cleo was on his way to Hawaii by use of his private jet. His jet is legend among his tight circle of business associates. His stewardesses flew only for him and were women he had met in Brazil and Cuba. They were educated women who were successful but poor by American standards. Their part—time stewardess job with Cleo tripled their annual earnings at home.

When in the mist of making a deal, the three stewardesses would be dressed as French maids, schoolgirls or nurses, all in skirts too small and tops overflowing with cleavage.

One hedge-fund guy and a stewardess actually performed the ultimate in excitement. Naked and entwined in each other's arms, they jumped from the plane, parachuting down to a private, white sand beach. They continued their lovemaking there, the waves wetting the sand, tickling them as the cold water ebbed and flowed beneath them. The sun warmed their skin and their hearts as their bodies pounded together. They experienced sexual nirvana.

Cleo was later to experience this stimulating adventure himself with Roxanne Du'brois. They had a torrid love affair that ended when she became pregnant. She wanted to have the baby; he did not. He resolved the dispute by stabbing her to death while she made love to him. He had her pregnant body cremated. The ashes of mother and unborn child were scattered on the same white sand beach, aided by a gentle breeze.

Today he is traveling with Tiffany so there will be no sexy stewardesses. She has never been to Hawaii. Her mother and father were lower-middle class, hard-working people from Oregon who later moved to Pennsylvania. She had decent parents. Her father liked to drink hard on weekends. He was quiet and honest. He did not have any ambition. If he did, he kept it to himself. Her mother was far too beautiful for the life she chose. She had few friends but seemed content. She loved her children and she tolerated her husband. He barely seemed to notice she was there except when he was drunk.

At those times, he would chase her around the house and tell her how beautiful she was. They seemed to live for these moments. That was the essence of their life together until one day when Tiffany was 13 her mother committed suicide. The night before her mother baked her apple pie and served it steaming hot with ice cream. She had given Tiffany a tight goodnight hug and watched television with her until midnight.

When Tiffany awoke, she found her mother under a white sheet and pink blanket, both stained red. A pillow lay atop her head with a hole where the 22-caliber slug entered her brain. The cop said it was unusual for a woman to kill herself using a gun. He said women almost never shoot near the face.

The insensitive bastard said, "She really musta wanted outa here." Tiffany never knew exactly why she did it. Her mother's note said simply. "I have lost the life I was meant to live and the grief of the loss has overwhelmed me."

Her father paid little attention to Tiffany after his wife's death. He became a full-time drunk and the booze that before made him amusing and frisky now made him bitter and mean.

Tiffany-Mercedes also wept for her mother and finding no support from her father looked to boys eager to exploit her grief. This only lasted for about a year but it was enough to give her a bad reputation in her small town.

She began to isolate. She talked less and less to her few good friends and went straight to her room when she got home. There she dreamt of far off and exotic places, of adventure, romance and of witty conversations with rugged individualist and clever rogues. The conversations in her head were better than the ones in her life. She was ready to leave. She applied to the University of Hawaii. She hoped it would be where the life of her dreams would begin. She had the grades and the potential for a scholarship.

But her father having nothing in his life hid her acceptance letter. He called the university and told admissions that she had been in a horrible accident and could not attend.

She did not want to go to any other college. In a few months, she loaded a backpack and took a plane to France. It began a journey of joy and sorrow that was her life until Cleo. She had slept in the streets of Milan and in penthouses in Paris. Yet her life's path had not provided time in Hawaii, the destination she dreamt of, in her room amidst despair. She did not know whether Hawaii would be the fulfillment of a childhood wish or the ultimate proof that dreams don't come true.

"TM, what do you think of the plane." Cleo asked as he took a seat beside her.

"I have always been fascinated by them. My mother and I used to watch them take off at the airport for hours at a time. I was fascinated by their power and I so wanted to fly to some mysterious destination."

A Chef inquires about their wishes for dinner.

She asks, "Do you have fat free cheese?"

Asking for fat free cheese is an insult to the French chef and she knew this from her years in Paris. She asked anyway because she has become accustomed to asking for exactly what she wants. The chef nods and goes to prepare the meal.

Cleo says, "You know, Tiffany, eating fat-free cheese is like having orgasm-free sex."

Elevating her leg to his lap, she tickles his abdomen with her toe and says, "If I did not eat the fat-free cheese, you would not like me enough to give me orgasms."

He says, "I don't know if that's true."

She turns surprised and says with sarcasm and humor "Do you mean you love my soul?"

"I mean you are more to me than the sum of your parts."

She kisses him on the neck and whispers in his ear. "So I am more than just a thing that gives you pleasure?" Although she is being playful and sexy, he hears the mocking tone in her voice.

He pulls away and says, "Yes, I don't understand why you would doubt that."

She sees that he is annoyed and tries to change the subject.

"Have you been to Hawaii before?" He looks at her intently before deciding to move on.

"Yeah Tiffany, I have been there a few times."

"What did you think?" she asked resuming her smile.

"I think that my money affords me islands that are more beautiful and less common. Although in my early years, it was the most beautiful place I had ever seen."

"How old were you?"

"I was 15. My brother came home from Vietnam. He had lost his legs and his mind. The conversations we had on the phone did not sound like him. He was at Tripler Army Hospital in Hawaii. I left my parents a letter and hitchhiked to California. I got a job working in the kitchen with one of the cruise lines, made it to Hawaii and went to see my brother."

"How was he?" She asked.

He hesitated for a moment and then answered, "My brother was my hero. He was smart, star of the football team, a ladies' man and life of the party."

"Sort of like you." She says.

"No", he says, "I worked hard to become what I am. He was a natural. I hardly ever saw him study or work out but he stayed in shape and was a great student. He always walked to the center of a crowded room and dated the prettiest girl. He was the man throwing the winning touchdown with ten seconds to go and if you knew my brother Bobby, you didn't have to see the ball caught. You could just close your eyes and wait for the cheers."

Tiffany says, "He sounds like quite a guy. Why didn't he go to college?"

Bloodworthy answers, "He thought military service was his duty but not to fight the commies or anything like that. Many of his friend's parents were finding ways for them to avoid the Army. He knew that the government had drafted many poor kids. He felt a responsibility to fight for the life and the nation he loved."

The pilot came on the intercom, "Sir we have run into some unexpected turbulence."

Bloodworthy continued. "Although no one would say it to my face, I heard people say he was dumb for going."

"They were probably afraid to go, so they would rather think he was dumb than think themselves cowards." She said trying to make it easier for him.

He continued, "Some of the parents thought he was brave and commended him. I stayed mostly in my room with my friends. I didn't say much to him before he left."

The plane was feeling now more like a subway train rocking through a tunnel than a corporate jet. Bloodworthy started to get up to talk to the pilot. She took his hand.

"Please finish." She said.

"As you might expect, he was a hero. He earned several medals, rose in rank and saved many lives. This was all before Tet."

"What?" she said, interrupting.

"The Tet Offensive. It was 1968 my brother was in Khe Sanh where the fighting was intensive for months. The angel that always seemed to be on his shoulder must have deserted him. His legs were blown off in the third month of fighting at that town."

"Is that when you went to see him?" she asked.

"No, I didn't go to see him for two years. My parents went." He is not looking directly at her anymore. "I didn't go because my parents didn't know what to expect and I was pretty young. Also, I was still mad at him for leaving me."

"Why were you mad at him?" Tiffany asks.

"I was a pretty rebellious kid. I never really got along with my parents. I always found them cold, distant and inauthentic. I mean I can't imagine them loving anything, except my brother Bobby but he was perfect."

"How did they react to seeing him?"

"They were still pale and bloodless after the nine-hour return trip. Bobby wasn't perfect anymore so they had nothing to love."

"When did you go?" She asked.

"As I said, I went two years later, on my fifteenth birthday. By then the hollow relationship with my parents had become a loathsome one.

At school, everyone was expecting me to be Bobby and I could not be. I became a loner. Eventually I wrote him. He acted like I had been writing all along, he wasn't mad at me but his letters showed how much he had changed."

The plane is now like a roller coaster. She grabs his arm. He uses the intercom to call the pilot, "Jeff, what the hell is going on?"

"Sir I can't escape the turbulence, Air traffic won't let me go beneath it and it gets worse the higher I go. I hope it won't be too much longer."

He looks at her "Remind me to get a new fucking pilot!"

She sees that he is agitated but wants him to continue. "How was it seeing your brother after all those years?"

"What?" He looks at her and after hesitating turns away

"It was hard to see him like that. It is hard to see the people you idolize get old and fat or lead ordinary lives. This was so much worse. This sucked the air out of my lungs. I could not understand how he could know the person he was and accept what he had become."

Tiffany gets tears in her eyes, she is suddenly thinking about her mother's suicide. She is tempted to tell him about it but does not.

"He seemed happy to see me and I tried not to look sad, tried to look him in the eye..." The pilot comes on.

"Mr. Bloodworthy There is a storm up ahead. We don't have enough gas to go back and there is nowhere to land. We are going to have to struggle through sir." The pilot's voice seemed shaky and they both notice.

She was both scared and excited by the danger. She had to know the answer to one question. "Is your brother still alive?"

"Yes, he medicates the pain in his head and his body with alcohol and pills but he is a sharp thinker and helps me from time to time."

She holds him tighter. She thinks Bobby is brave, still an exceptional man and thinks her mother was weak for leaving her. She then felt guilty for thinking her mother weak. The plane jumps hard. They both realize how serious the danger could be.

She asks, "Have you been in a plane before when things were this bad?"

He decides to lie to her to make her feel safer. "Sure I have, quite a few times." She knows he is lying but appreciates that he is trying to calm her.

She says, "So were you also lying when you told me that I was not just another pretty face?"

They are now beginning to see lightening in an increasingly dark sky. "I always want more of you," Cleo says. Their dangerous flight and her feelings of abandonment by her mother make her less guarded.

"You know how you felt as a kid when your brother left you, that is how I have felt for most of my life, only worse. I feel as if I can't let myself love too much because I can't stand the heartbreak of being left again."

He looks at her and knows what she wants to hear and knows he will say it even though he does not feel it completely yet.

"I will never leave you. You can trust me with your heart. Promise me that you will not hold back. You must give me everything. I need you to love me with all your might. If you do this, you will always be able to rely on me. You must trust me with the blood that runs through your veins and the breath that gives you life. Do you give me the essence of your love? Do you give me your soul?"

She nods. The plane now is shaking, rattling as if it is going to burst apart. He yells above the noise of the plane.

"I must hear it. Will you give me your soul?"

"Yes.", she screams as tears run down the cheeks of her doe-like eyes. It is completely dark now in the cabin of the plane. Her head is tossed. It hits a window and she passes out.

Chapter 4

Noble Cronkite arrives late to work. He walks slowly as if it is the last mile and his desk is the electric chair. He has a hangover from last night; a Tuesday evening spent at home cursing the tv and drinking scotch. He sits down and immediately takes a bite out of the pastrami sandwich he was saving for lunch. He opens a cup of hot black coffee from a thin, cheap cup. When he picks it up, he burns his fingers and he spills coffee on his keyboard.

"Maybe that will add some heat to your writing, Cronk."

Noble gives Stu Hobson an annoyed look and says, "Cute. We know you are all heat and no light"

Cronk uses his handkerchief to soak the liquid from the keyboard. Hobbs flashes a crooked smile and says, "So is that what passes for wit in your circle? So how is that group of dinosaurs that used to rule the earth and how long before you are all extinct?"

"What are you talking about?" Noble asks.

"You know what I mean, the dozen of you that get together at Le Plume and talk about how there is no real news anymore."

Noble replies, "Oh you mean real newsmen. Yeah, we are an endangered species, hardly see us anymore."

"No one wants to see you. You are all boring robots and way too ugly for television. You're sort of like silent movie stars before the talkies."

Noble responds, "Websites, mousse and whiter teeth are the only contributions that you and your girlfriends have made to journalism. Our corporate masters own the once free press and they won't pay for investigative journalism. You glorified weather-girls enable them with your total lack of curiosity, acumen or integrity."

"Ooh, nice words, too bad you can't put them together in a way that anybody cares about. Ratings baby ratings. I love them and they love me. I am a household name and you are two years from being a trivia question. Enjoy what's left of your coffee and your career." Stu Hobson walks away.

Noble is pissed and his head is pounding, two parts hangover, one part Stu. It was his anxiety de jour.

"Don't let him get to you." Steve said from his desk.

"No worries." Noble said giving him a weak smile.

Steve like Stu is a poor newsman but he is clueless. He really thinks what he does is good news. He is a good guy though, the hooker with a heart of gold.

Steve continued "Stu is just letting the fame go to his head. I always thought you were-uh you are one of the best. When I received an honorary degree from Arizona, I got several questions asking what it was like working with you."

Steve smiles and continues. "Remember when I first started working here and I would follow you around like a little puppy dog."

"Yeah I remember." Noble said. I remember losing the co-anchor spot to this rookie. He thought.

Steve continued, "Two Pulitzer prizes one at the Times and one with Knight-Rider, that's like winning two Super-Bowl rings from two different teams. You are a legend, Cronk." He pats Noble on the back and heads toward the newsroom.

Noble wonders whether Hobbs or Steve made him feel worse. Hobbs thought he was a dinosaur, Steve thought he was some kind of living statue. He needed a big story, one that would make life feel like a first kiss instead of a long line at the supermarket. But all he got nowadays were occasional features and human-interest stories. He felt like he was a Greeter at Wal-Mart.

He had not been a real reporter for many years. He thought the move to cable news would give him a more energized audience. He thought that he would bring integrity to 24-hour news and for a while, they did things his way.

Instead of asking two angry people with opposing views what they thought of a topic or looping the same news, he gave listeners substance. He explained what was at stake, the history of the issue, who it would help and hurt. He had follow-ups for weeks so people knew the process and how everything was resolved. Instead of news being an inch high and a mile wide, news had depth and research.

It was more important to him to inform the public. It trumped sensationalism and cost cutting. Unfortunately ratings fell. Management began making "suggestions" and then demands.

The public was slow to adjust to the change His urgings to the network for more time went unheeded. The voices in the organization who had argued against his version of the news gained strength because of his failure. News as low cost entertainment won, good pictures, good people and good night. That is cable news. I have only myself to blame he thought, I joined a brothel thinking that if the conversation was good enough no one would fuck me.

"Cronk, got one for you." An assistant producer says.

"What is it?" Noble asked

"Take a look, I got to get going." The assistant left. Noble gave a quick, silent prayer for a good story.

He said, "Damn." snatched up the note in anger and disappointment and stormed out.

Joe was walking. He had lost ten pounds since his vision at the police station. He decided to fast until he made progress on his mission from the father. As a Homeless man, he was dependent on soup kitchens and scraps, so his "fasting" was more a decision not to look for food than it was much of a change in eating habits. The weight loss came from Joe's walking. He walked everywhere, even running frantically at times if he surmised that he should be cross-town for clues to finding the cave of the vampire.

He is standing across the street from a bank when two men exit. Both men have taken hostages. They have guns drawn and their arms around the necks of the women. The thieves step backwards, turning their heads from side to side.

One woman is screaming and crying. The other woman is frozen in fear and tears are flowing from her unblinking eyes. John Doe moves immediately thinking this crisis is related to what he must do. As he walks toward them, the gunmen see him and one of them shakes the gun at him and says, "Get the fuck out of here."

He continues to walk in their direction and in a voice barely audible, he says, "Go and sin no more."

One bandit shoots at him twice and his hostage screams more loudly and begins trying to wiggle out of his grasp. She pushes hard and is almost free. He shoots at Joe again and misses. The woman is free. The other gunman shoots at Doe and his gun misfires. Click, click, click.

They hear sirens. The driver yells from the car.

"We gotta go, now!" The second gunman throws his hostage to the ground and they both get in the car and take off. Almost immediately afterwards police cars arrive. As the first cars screech to the curb, the hostages point in the direction of the fleeing getaway car. Two more police cars appear, then a third and fourth, then the SWAT truck. A crowd has gathered and traffic begins to back up in both directions.

Police place barricades on the sidewalk and position cops to steer traffic away from the chaos. Police have entered the bank and the hostages are in an ambulance with a detective.

The story of the robbery is beginning to unfold. Noble Concrite is the first reporter on the scene. He was on his way to cover yet another human-interest story when he stumbled on to the robbery. He saw the mysterious stranger walk toward men with loaded guns. He saw him console the hostages and walk away as soon as he heard the sirens. Noble had to think quickly. He knew he had to choose between following this man and being the first reporter to interview the hostages. He knew that even if he got an exclusive with the hostages it would not last. All the other reporters would descend on them in moments and by the end of the week, no one would know or care who was first. No this guy was the story. He would follow him. First, he did something that he learned from young reporters, he yelled at the small crowd that now gathered.

"Hey, I will pay $500 to anybody that caught the robbery on your camera phone."

He looks around, one guy holds up his phone. He motions for the guy to come with him. The guy hesitates. He says to him, "I just want to copy it; you can still keep the video and make the 500."

The guy hurries toward him. He tells the guy to wait in his car and hurries to catch up to the stranger.

"Hey wait up." He moves quickly and is almost out of breath as he reaches him.

"Please stop. I feel like I am going to have a heart attack."

Joe slows down, looks back, and sees a man with his hands on his knees breathing heavily. His eyes are bulging and his face is flush. Doe turns around and walks back toward him. Noble straightens up and straightens his ten-year-old tie.

He sticks out his hand and says, "I'm Noble." Joe shakes his hand.

"J C Doe, God bless you. Can I do anything to help you?" Joe says.

"Yes you can. I saw what you did. It was amazing and I have a guy waiting in my car that saw the whole thing. I am a reporter Noble Croncite."

He waits for Doe to recognize him or his name, when that does not happen he continues. "You are a hero my friend and I want everyone to know what a brave thing you have done here today." Doe just looks at him, withdrawing slightly.

"I want to take you and Gregory, the guy with the camera phone, to my office and I want to interview you. Look don't worry I will walk you through the whole thing, it really is quite painless."

J.C. Doe's first reaction is to say no but he feels that all of this may be a clue to performing the task that God has given him, so he agrees and says, "I will follow you."

They head back to the car and Gregory is impatient. He says, "I really have to go. Can I just send it to your phone?"

Noble is confused. He asks, "Can you do that?"

"Of course."

He eyes Noble and says, "You do have a cell phone don't you?" Noble did have a cell phone and a laptop but only knew how to do the most basic things with either one.

He reaches over to his canvas bag and produces one. Greg sees the laptop in the bag and says he will send it to his computer after he is paid.

Noble writes a check and Greg says, "I should charge you extra for this."

He then opens it for him. Noble gives him a business card and Greg writes down his name and telephone number. He then focuses on Doe who has been sitting in the back of the car.

"Come on up front." he says.

Noble has been moving so fast since he stumbled upon the robbery that he is just now observing the "hero" that he will soon present to the world. Doe although clean still smells, his hair is long and unkempt. He is dressed in toga tied at the waist with long gray pants and sandals.

He is exceptionally thin with penetrating eyes. His fingers are long as are his nails.

"Would you like to get something to eat?" He asks Joe Doe.

Joe nods, and then asks, "Can we get fish and soup, I have just finished fasting and I would like that very much."

Noble says "Sure."

He begins to think of restaurants. He decides to go to a place in the Village where the food is good and no one will care how he is dressed. They arrive and sit. Croncite is about to begin the interview. He tells Doe that everything he says will be recorded and takes out a recording device.

"Interview with Joe C Doe, Mr. Doe please tell me about the robbery. How did you first notice it?"

"I was walking down Third Ave and 89th street when I saw two women with arms around their neck being taken out of the bank by two men with guns."

"What did you do?"

"I went across the street to ask the gunmen to release the ladies."

"So you crossed the street and when you were on the same block as the gunmen you were about seven car lengths away is that right."

"Yes."

"And did they see you as soon as you crossed the street."

"Yes, very soon after."

"Did they point their guns at you?"

"Yes, first both of them did and then one pointed his gun at me while the other covered the hostages and the bank entrance."

"How did the women look; were they frightened?"

"Of course, they looked terrified."

"What did you do next?"

"I began to walk toward them and pray."

"So you walked toward the two bank robbers, one with a loaded gun pointed right at you?"

"Yes."

"Were you afraid?"

"No."

"No, why not?"

"Faith." He replied.

"You had faith that the bullets would not hit you?"

"No I knew that I was doing the will of God. I had faith that whatever happened would be best for me. Either I would be with my father in heaven or he would use me to help others. Either fate was equally acceptable to me, neither was frightening."

Noble looked at him in disbelief. He looked into his eyes and did not know if Doe believed what he said because he was crazy or out of a devout faith but he was sure that Doe believed it.

"Then did one of them fire at you?"

"Yes."

"What happened?" Joe looks from one shoulder to the other.

"He missed."

Noble asks, "When you saw him shoot, when the gun fired, did that scare you?"

"I was startled, it passed near my ear."

"Did you ever think about running or taking cover?"

Doe asks Noble "Do you have children?"

"Uh yes." Noble replies.

"Would you run away if your child had a gun to his head like these women?"

"I hope not." Concrite says.

"It is no different." Joe replies.

Noble can't believe what he is hearing but he knows this interview is gold.

"He fired again, didn't he?"

"Yes."

"But you kept coming."

"Yes".

"Then the second gunman tried to fire at you but his gun jammed."

"No weapon formed against me can prosper."

"And then you reached the gunman, what happened?"

"One woman freed herself and the other was tossed to the ground. I think they heard the police sirens and left."

"What did you do next?"

"I took the hands of the two women and told them 'God loves them and that they were safe.' Then I left."

"Why did you leave?"

"I want to eat; I haven't had a hot meal in some time."

"Sure of course."

He pats Joe on the back and walks toward the men's room. He is elated. He thinks this guy may be the second coming of his career.

After their meal, Noble pays for a hotel room for Joe. He also gives him money for clothes and a haircut. He then heads for the office. He needs to see the news.

Chapter 5

Cleo Bloodworthy has interrupted his vacation to speak to a group of new upper and elite managers. They are in New York eagerly awaiting his speech. Each new manager has signed an agreement stating that he will not disclose the contents of the speech and knows that he will be terminated if he does. Executives who have went to other companies and revealed the secrets of the speech have mysteriously disappeared. Their disappearance is generally attributed to bad luck but only adds to the legend of the speech. Cleo is relaxed and full of vigor. He enjoys enlightening new minds. He has joked that this is his missionary work and that he is recruiting new souls for capitalism.

"Greetings Captains of capital. I welcome you to Reversal' and congratulate you on your choice. You are here today because you have been judged as exceptional businessmen and leaders and because you have special qualities that fit the Reversal' mission and vision.

"I know that you are exceptional because of your days of testing, unfettered observation, and interviews. My system is flawless, as a result, my businesses thrive, and my companies' executives are extremely rich.

"Today we pay homage to the root of our prosperity. Not to money or power, no that is the fruit. The foundation, my new friends, of all that we love, is perception. It is perception that propels markets to glorious heights or to the depths of despair. If the emperor is naked but everyone says he is clothed, the emperor gets richer and richer. If someone yells, "The emperor has no clothes." Markets collapse and business suffer. If we do not control perception governments, instead of being our weak, greedy partner, will want to flex its muscle. If we lose control of perception, the peasants will be banging at the door of the castle wielding torches and pitchforks. They will want to take your riches and steal food from your mouth.

"Today, we the new emperors, have more weapons at our disposal. We have Industrial psychologist, researchers, brain studies, sociologist, advertisers and actuaries who can help us induce our ideas into their brains. We can know what music, colors, experiences and characteristics will make the peasants buy, but still that is not enough. We must use our new weapons to create love for business, so that no matter what we do, the people will not storm the castle demanding our heads.

"Henry Ford once famously said, 'I pay my workers well so they can afford to buy my products.' Well, we don't need them now. Workers are cheaper elsewhere. We have India, China, and we have buyers all over the globe. More importantly, the stock market is no longer tied to industry, its wealth is self-generating. You must remember our greatest product is wealth. If making a good quality product creates more wealth, good. If cutting workers and quality makes wealth ,then good. Quality of product, workers, or the product itself are disposable variables. Your goal line is quarterly earnings. Your mission is money.

"More than this, we must control any perception that is even tangentially related to business. We must embrace political, religious and social ideas that protect the perceptions that make us rich. Our patriotism must be the kind that supports war profiteering and huge defense spending. We must embrace a nationalism that blindly loves

America and the troops. Our greatest heroes must be soldiers and policemen.

"We must embrace the culture of terror so that the frightened masses will allow excessive defense spending to be safe from the enemy abroad. We must create fear of immigrants, Blacks and the poor, the internal enemy. We must have our politicians create laws that limit rights of citizens and protect property. Capitalism will be the great rescuer that will provide the gated communities and private schools that will insulate them from their fears. Politicians will dare not cut defense spending or attack business, fearing loss of their career or risking their party's anger.

"Your church must love the military and bless the wars. They must be against the interest of the poor and think the poor are only poor because they are lazy, genetically inferior and don't believe in Christ. The masses must always look down when there is a problem, never up.

"When we kill hundreds of thousands with our weapons, they will not complain about the use of our weapons, they will not even pray for the babies killed in war, they will cry only those babies that have been aborted and be willing to kill abortionists. This must be your church. You must condemn any atheist or Christian who believes differently. It is this form of Christianity that got us through Slavery and the Indians Wars.

"We stole the land and labor and the church blessed us and called them ungodly savages. We must embrace Conservative Christianity. It is the religion of nationalism and wealth.

"Your media must also be corporate and conservative. That means totally business-friendly, say no to investigative reporting, yes to fearmongering and race baiting. The people watching news must be afraid or angry, emotional, never rational.

"Education must be termed elitist and liberal. The people must see their ignorance as wholesome and moral. The peasants must rely on our politicians, our media, our religious leaders and their beer-drinking buddies for their opinions. They must not think critically. If they denigrate us, it must feel like they have committed a sin. If they march against us, it must feel like treason. They must be ready to kill to save our lower taxes and call socialist those who would fight for their higher wages.

"So my friends, you are not joining a business, you are evangelist for prosperity. You must remember always to promote the ideas that guarantee our success. You must control perception."

Tiffany enters the room. She is wearing a bikini tailored to cling to her every curve. He was grateful to have found a woman both perfect and perfect for him. Yet he also resented the increasing control she had over his thoughts and his feelings. So at times, he treated her aggressively. At these times, she would never show fear or hurt. Instead, she displayed a certainty that he would never really harm her. She knew her value.

"Are you ready for me or should I go alone?" She said smiling slyly and posing seductively.

He called her bluff, "I have some more business to take care of. I can meet you for dinner. Why don't you scout out a good restaurant?"

She put on a thin straw hat, with a brim that had as many curves as she had. She walked slowly to the door, gave him a wry smile and said, "We'll see."

As soon as she left, Cleo took out a vial of blood and drank it in front of the mirror. He let the blood ooze from the corner of his lips and snarled, baring his blood drenched teeth. He felt powerful. His lust for blood was growing. Soon after tasting human blood for the first time, he began experimenting with other blood types. He tried cow, lamb and even moved on to wolf, rat and deer.

He tried different combinations but nothing thrilled him as much as the pig and human blood cocktail. He had established a connection at the blood bank for getting blood. It was not much of a problem for a man with so much money. He also managed to remain anonymous by having someone pick up the blood and leave it at a designated location.

At times, he worried about diseases from drinking the blood of pigs and the other animals he experimented with but nothing ever seemed to happen to him. This added to questions he had about why he was so different. Were there many others like him? He wondered. So he started searching the Internet. He did genetics testing, used Ancestry.com and joined the blogs of organizations catering to strange fetishes. He joined cults that used blood sacrifice.

He found the genetics interesting and he did find anomalies in his genes. The organizations online were mostly people infatuated with books or movies that popularized atypical practices. The cults were powerful and dark. He became convinced of a dark power by the very real evil that some of these groups were capable of evoking. He used their techniques and rituals against his enemies and achieved limited success. Yet they were no help in his quest for self-discovery.

Ancestry.com revealed that his ancestors were accused of being Vampires. He was equally surprised to find others that were very successful men.

The earliest record of any distinction was as a member of the Poor Knights of Christ and the Temple of Solomon commonly known as the Knights of Templar. The Knights were a Christian military organization that fought in the Crusades and distinguished itself as the pre-eminent financial innovator and power broker of the time. After combat and modest financial success, his ancestor and his Saxon wife moved to Romania in the 12th century. His middle-eastern hue was strange to Romanians. He was tested by word and by sword but he won all battles.

He had wealth earned in war and finance. He and his family lived out their life in peace and prosperity.

There was not a relative of any note again until Lord Afanasii. He was a noble, highly favored by the prince. In the 15th century, he fought in the war against the Ottoman Empire. He fought for the Prince of Wallachia and for Christianity. The Prince Vlad was legendary to his people for his fierce prowess on the battlefield and later on the pages of Bram Stokers Dracula.

The third relative of note was his Great-grandfather. He knew of his great-grandfathers life during the Great Depression. He was the man that built a minor fortune into a major one and then lost it. He was the reason Cleo's father needed to start from scratch to re-build his wealth.

He was proud of this lineage and it validated all of his feelings and his philosophy of life. In fact, his hobby become researching his friends, business partners and employees. He had replaced successful managers because of distant cousins who were failures.

He had not researched Tiffany's background. He wanted to know so he paid an agency to do it. He had just never dared to look. He had brought the envelope with him. He took it out of his attaché case and threw it on the bed. He looked at the bed and tried to imagine never having Tiffany-Mercedes on it again. The thought sent a chill up his spine and made his brow damp with sweat. He planned to ask her to marry him. He could not let his future generations down. He agonized over it, he picked up and put it down but in the end, he could not do it. He threw the envelope back on the bed and took a shower.

Chapter 6

Using all the tools at his disposal, Noble had convinced the producers to add a full seven-minute interview with Joe Doe. There was a lot of resistance. They thought the robbery segment was already too long. "Trust me." Concrite kept saying but they were long past trusting his instincts. What ultimately convinced them is that no one else had Joe, making the interview an exclusive.

There is one minute to air. Concrite reassures Joe. "Look Joe, just relax. Just think as If it is the two of us in the restaurant."

Joe says, "I am fine."

Joe wonders if this will help him with his mission from God. He is about to ask Noble if he can ask anyone if they know the cave of which God spoke but he waits too late.

"5,4,3,2,1 you're on the air."

"Good evening, tonight we have an SLD exclusive. We have the man who helped to save the hostages at the bank today. He is a man who is fearless and harmless, wise and humble. He is someone who will sacrifice himself to save others and wants no reward for his services.

"To avoid fame or praise he insists on using the name Joe. But you will see this is no ordinary Joe. Joe how are you today?"

"I am blessed and thankful."

"Joe by now everyone has seen the film of your heroic effort. The hostages from the bank now identified as Grace and Lois have tearfully thanked you for saving them. Joe let me show you the tape."

He points to a screen where Lois, a young, thin, brunette bank teller whose large pretty eyes are full with impending tears and her voice is trembling with emotion.

"He just walked toward the gun. The bullets were inches from him but he didn't stop. The gunmen got confused, which allowed me to get loose. I have never seen such a selfless act, never."

Grace who had been nodding the whole time spoke, "He was so calm and kind. After saving us he was so reassuring, I was a nervous wreck. I couldn't stop crying and screaming. They would have killed me for sure but after talking with him, I was ok. It was like he gave me his energy or something."

Noble Cronkite continued. "I know you don't like to be called a hero but that's what you are. What were you thinking as you approached the bank robbers?"

"I thought these women needed help and I am going to help them."

"No hesitation no thought for your own safety."

"I am always safe when I am doing God's will."

"So the bullets are literally whizzing past your ear and still you go forward, did you think you might die?"

"I thought that if I live, I will help others as God intends for us to do. I thought that if I die I will be with the father and what could be better than that?" Joe smiles.

Noble could see his producers telling him he had 30 seconds left and he wanted to personalize the interview? The guy seemed too much like a religious whacko, so he asked,

"Tell us a little about yourself, are you married, do you have children?"

Joe answered, "They say that everyone has 15 minutes of fame, if this is mine I don't want to spend it on myself. I want to tell everyone to remember God in your everyday life, when you go to work and speak to your children and ask always, what would Jesus do? Pray in thanks and ask for forgiveness. It will remind you of your blessing and keep you humble. Nothing outside you is greater than the light you have within you. Feed the light."

Noble sees that he is out of time. "Thank you. Back to you Stu."

He thanked Joe and paid him a few hundred for the interview. He had previously arranged for Joe to stay in Westchester with a friend so that he could reach Joe if there was a need. He would also be secluded from other reporters trying to get an interview.

Noble is only mildly pleased with the interview. He had hoped to make Joe a guy the average man could relate to. Instead, he feared people would dismiss Joe as a fringe character.

"Noble, Noble." Racine said as she ran toward him.

"That was a wonderful interview. Mr. Doe I loved the things you said." She hugged Noble and shook Joe's hand. Noble gave her a smile. He knew it was not a great interview but her enthusiasm was contagious.

"You were incredible. This will put you on top again and America will get real news again."

She looked at him, exuberant, eyes dancing, intelligent and bursting with youthful energy. She idolized him. She studied him in college and crafted her style of journalism to be like his.

He thought sometimes that she would make a good mate for him. He sensed she had a real crush on him. She was a frequent lunch companion. She touched him all the time, sometimes the touches would linger. Other times he thought she saw him as a textbook paragraph come to life, a walking talking figure from a wax museum. Anyway a sexual encounter would just make him ordinary, he thought, a middle-aged guy with a large belly who couldn't compare to the youngsters.

"Hey Noble." Croncrite turns his head. It is Stu Hobson.

"Maybe you can get your guy to pray for you to get an interesting story. God works miracles." He walks off laughing.

Racine gives Stu a stern look and says to Noble, "If there was any justice he would be hawking products for $19.95." Noble grins.

"I'm going to get Joe settled and head over to Le Plume this evening. Would you like to come?"

Racine was ecstatic. She smiled broadly and then hugged him tightly. She let go and held his hand.

"What time?" She asked

"Promptly at eight." He said.

He had known Racine for two years and this was her first invitation to the circle of mostly older distinguished journalist. Seating at the long black table at the end of the l-shaped bar and restaurant was restricted. It was by invitation of a member and with the consent of the group. They were once the most influential men and women in news .Now they were more like refuges plotting a revolution.

Their enemy had endless streams of wealth and the microphones, their scepters of power. There were seven seated at the table when Noble and Racine arrived. None of them needed any introduction. All were well-known or critical successes in the industry. Dave from PBS, Sal from the New Yorker, Mark from the Times and James, retired from the Post. The only other woman there is Christie, a researcher who had provided the foundation for many stories for the men at the table and Rosalind, a legendary editor from Knight-Rider. The other TV people were from 60 minutes and two were from National Public Radio.

Racine was a little intimidated. Sal was already talking.

"Did you see the idiot on CNN last night. All those guys are is graphics and grins. He goes to the experts and asks 'What do you think about the town hall meetings?' None of this has anything to do with health care. If they wanted to inform people about that, they would tell people that all organizations of doctors and nurses prefer single payer. The majority of Americans in survey after survey prefer single payer..."

Dave says, "What gets me is that they keep saying it's liberals who want it, not doctors, nurses and most Americans. So if you don't like liberals, you don't like single payer."

Rosalind says, "What astounds me is all this attention to these nuts on the right, these Tea Badgers, or Mad Hatters, whatever they're called. When millions of people around the world and hundreds of thousands in America, flooded the streets to protest the war in Iraq, CNN gave it 10 seconds on Headline News and downplayed the numbers."

Noble and Racine are seated and Noble is talking to the waiter and trying to get Racine's attention so she can order. She is riveted by the discussion. He nudges Racine again. She orders a tuna wrap and a salad.

Mark takes a bite of his corned beef sandwich and with mustard hanging from his mustache bellows.

"They're scared of Wolf. They are so afraid of being called liberal they will televise any fruitcake with an opposing point of view. You know like this: 'The left says that raping one year one girls is wrong. What do you say?"

A few of them laugh. Mark goes back to his sandwich.
James voice has softened over the years, so the others quiet down when he speaks.

"I hear you Mark, that's true but nothing has hurt our calling like the filth of money. When news was a public service, a loss leader, these guys in broadcast news never had to worry about ratings and advertisers. News was not expected to turn a profit. It was a public service. You didn't have to rock the crowd; you just had to tell the truth.

If there was a good cause like civil rights, you could show dogs and water hoses being turned on people and let the images speak for themselves. Now there is no right and wrong, no issue that is judged on its merit. Like you said the questions would more likely have been: 'Is freedom good for Negro's?' or on Wolf 'Should communist and domestic terrorist be shot?' 'Are the police too lenient?"

Dave spoke again, "Yes, we were the ones who spoke truth to power, the voice of the average citizen struggling to understand an ever more complex and changing world. We informed, we didn't equivocate. We were moral vanguards, not pitchmen. As we stand by helplessly, there is a whole generation of youth that will think this is news, the same way they think Judge Judy is the justice system."

Rosalind was playing with her wine glass. She added, "Most of the foreign news bureaus are gone. Investigative journalism cost too much for the corporate guys and of course corporate news never takes a stand on anything. They are afraid they will be sued. Good newspapers have died and others are dying. The people have no voice except maybe the internet but where does that leave us."

The busboys were clearing the plates and the waiter was asking about desert. Noble, who was involved in side conversations and making Racine feel comfortable said to everyone,

"Before we go I wanted to formally introduce Racine." She smiled, nodded, and shook hands. Mark spoke from behind the mustard stained cloth napkin he used to wipe his face.

"Do you have any thoughts on the discussion?" He asked Racine.

Racine had intended to remain silent and just listen. She had a lot she wanted to say but did not want to seem pushy.

"Well", she said, looking at James, the senior member of the group, "Money and ratings are here to stay. There is no going back. Our problem seems to be how to market broccoli so well that people prefer it to ice cream."

Sal said somberly, "Yeah, that's exactly right."

A few of the journalist were about to leave but heard the beginning of a discussion that could have wings.

James said, "Any ideas on how we do that?"

Racine had thought about this ever since Noble lost his show. She knew what a great loss his show was to the culture and mission of journalism but she also knew it was not coming back, not that or anything like it.

"You ever see those breakfast cereals with a popular character, lots of colors, lots of sugar and stuff that is not even food but the product is fortified with vitamins. We have to sneak the vitamins in."

James says, "The problem with that is these added vitamins are the poorest way for the body to get vitamins. There is some doubt that the body even processes them at all."

Christie the researcher spoke up. "James the truth is that if Americans didn't get their nutrition from junk, they wouldn't get any. As abundant as oranges and vegetables are, we don't eat them.

"Americans get most of their vitamin C from French fries. A horrible choice, full of fat, grease and additives and very little vitamin C but we eat it. We eat it a lot."

Sal says, "It's like Jazz. The number of people listening to this beautiful, complex music had become so few that Jazz musicians couldn't make a living. There were Jazz greats who had to put aside their rather large egos and play with five other greats just to fill up the small venues. Then Jazz fusion came, it was marketable, it got a larger audience. It was simple and melodic. Gone was the improvisation, the artistry but it introduced a larger number of people to Jazz and the real jazzmen got some record sales and gigs. But I tell you Racine I don't know if it helped or it hurt. To most people fusion is now Jazz."

Chris from NPR asked, "Isn't that what cable news is now, entertainment and excitement with a little news thrown in?"

"Yeah, it started off as making the news more exciting. Now if it ain't exciting, it ain't news." Mark adds.

Dave says, "It reminds me of something I read about some spider. The female, which is dominant, bites off the head of the male during the act of sex. After thousands of years of evolution, the male wises up. It creates a web and puts a little bit of food in it. While the female is unraveling the food, he has his fun and gets away." Some laugh, some smile.

"Wait it gets better. After a few thousand years more, the male leaves out the food, he just does the web. She gets no food but she still tears away at the web, that's conditioning." They all laugh. "That's the news today, you're fucked, you don't get nothing out of it but you keep looking, hoping that there will be something nourishing like there once was"

"Sal is excited "If we can sneak some food back in the web, viewers won't go back to life without it. Is that the premise?"

Mark belches "Yeah."

"I'm not convinced this will work." Dave says looking directly at Racine. "I do agree that we need to again try to restore the news to its' rightful place. I think we all have been a little gun shy after our last effort. I hope we have learned from our mistakes.

"I want to use the tactic that's on the table but unless we have a solid strategy for reclaiming values, we are doomed to fail. We must, to use the metaphor, put something in the web more broadly. We must use media to put morality back in culture, critical thinking back in education and love back in family. We must put the golden rule back in religion and we must ask Americans to share risks and prosperity in our democracy. They have the power, money and momentum but like the martial arts, we will use their power and their strength against them."

Noble answers his vibrating cell phone. He has been ignoring it. He knew it was SLD but he was willing to wait until after the meeting. This time it was the producer's number he saw in the phone. He picked up.

"Noble." He said.

"Noble, get down here now. We got faxes, twitters, e-mails and phones all at full blast!"

Noble says, "What, why?

The producer answers, "It's your guy, Joe Blow, Doe or whatever. Guys think he is Rambo, women want to marry him, churches want him to speak and politicians want pictures with him. This guy has got it. Is he somewhere safe? How long can we keep him exclusive? I'm gonna give you some support on this one. Bring him home baby, bring him home."

Noble is astonished, he then thinks his first instincts were right. He just got a little afraid. He nudges Racine who is now the focal point of the discussion. He nudges her again, this time more forcefully. In a loud whisper, he urges, "Come with me, its urgent."

He guides her to a quiet corner and tells her the news. She resists the urge to hug him in such a public place. "Noble, I'm so happy for you. I told you he was a killer interview."

"Thanks Rae, but it's not me. This guy has got something. He is special, I mean once in lifetime stuff. I felt it when I first saw him then I lost confidence after the interview. I told myself the interview was no good."

He paused, then grabbed her hand and said, "Let's get out of here, we can analyze me later."

Racine said, "Wait, I think this guy may be the one we have been talking about, a way back into the game. Let's tell the others what's happening."

Croncite said emphatically, "No. Those are still news people. Anyone of them would tail us to get to Joe for their own newspapers or networks if they knew how big he is. Don't be fooled, everyone will want this story and access to Joe. You and I can work out a plan on how to use this guy for the greater good but first he is ours."

Racine could see his face fill with primal energy. He had the scent. He was an animal seeking its prey. He was beyond convincing. "Okay." She said, "We will bring them in later."

Chapter 7

J.C. Doe leaves Noble's safe house in Westchester and heads to the Lower East Side of Manhattan. He has made it as far as the South Bronx and is making his way to the bridge. He is alert. His homeless life has taught him to avoid side streets and deserted areas. He walks down 149th street observing people shopping at stores or engaging vendors. There is much commerce and little of the gangs, violence and jeopardy of a decade ago.

He is no longer invisible. He receives a few puzzled looks by people trying to remember where they have seen his face. A group of teenage girls pass him, one points, jabs her finger in the air and tells the others that he is the guy that was on the news. He nods.

"Hey my friend, I have nice CDs and sunglasses for you my friend. Come look." The African vendor beckons him. He turns his head smiles and politely says no.

When Joe turns back around a woman is inches from his face and she is screaming, "You are him. Help me, help me."

Her eyes are bulging and bloodshot. Her nails are long and cracked and her hair is wild. She is unstable. She looks terrified. She is shaking like she is about to explode. In her aching, pleading voice, he hears the remnants of past horrors.

She drops to her knees. She grabs him, still pleading. She is oblivious to her nails digging into his wrist. He tries to lift her to her feet but she fears he is trying to push her away. She grabs his leg with both hands, imploring him.

"You are the only one who can help me, don't leave me."

She is screaming and a small crowd is beginning to gather to watch. He tries to reassure her that he will not leave and urges her to stand.

Out of the corner of his eye, he sees two men dodging traffic and racing across the street. The first man reaches them and pushes Joe causing him to fall.

"Shevonne, what's going on?" He grabs her arm as she clings desperately to Joe's leg.

"Don't hurt him." she yells and tries to bite the man's hand.

He lets go, looks at Joe, and says, "Oh shit you the dude from the police station! Come on baby, this dude is crazy."

He uses more force and unclenches her hands from around Joe's leg. Joe stands up and yells, "Wait I must talk to you."

The man sees a police car turn the corner. Shevonne is yelling while the man drags her. "I won't leave unless he comes with us."

The man keeps looking at the approaching police car. It is two blocks away and the car has not turned on its' siren yet. "Okay, okay, he can come but we have to get the hell out of here."

He releases her and says, "Everybody smile like we having a good old time."

They walk across the street. The man and his friend laugh while Joe and Shevonne display fixed awkward smiles on their face. The police car passes by them slowly but does not stop.

The man, still smiling says, "Let's go into the store. If we go to the car, they might run the plates. I don't need no more trouble."

The second man says, "I'm hungry, Lets go to Burger King." After waiting on a long line, they order some food.

The man looks at Joe and says, "You're treating, motherfucker." Joe understands that it is not a question or suggestion and pulls out some money.

The second man said, "Oh, he's treating. I didn't know that shit. Let me get three more Whoppers and two large fries."

When the food is ready, the man instructs Joe, to go outside, look around, and see if there are any cops there.

"Don't be obvious and shit, act like you waiting for somebody."

Joe follows instructions and reports that the cops are gone. They go to the car and head for Shevonne's house, which is nearby. She is in the car next to Joe, holding his hand and rocking back and forth in the seat. During the ride Joe learns that the man's name is Cleverness. The second man is Gerard, Cleverness calls him "G". When they arrive at the apartment Shevonne is still clinging on to Joe.

"Let the man go, Shevonne, so y'all can fit in the door."

She doesn't listen, so Joe turns sideways so they can both fit in the door. They plop on the couch together and Shevonne stares intently at

Joe. The apartment is messy and has an odor of old clothes and rancid food.

"Damn Shevonne, what the fuck smells in here? I pay your little brother twenty dollars a week to clean this place up and it smells like old walrus dick in here. When is the last time he been by?" Shevonne shrugs her shoulders and looks back at Joe.

"Well he better get over here or give back my money. Just cause he's your brother don't mean I won't put my foot up his ass."

He puts down his burger "Damn, it stinks so bad it here I can't eat my food." He throws it on the table. G looks up. He is finishing his second Whopper.

He stuffs a load of fries in his mouth and says, "That shit don't bother me. You don't want it, I'll eat it." and adds it to his pile.

Cleverness smiles and says, "Damn G, "You would fucking eat rat fat in a sewer if they fried it and put it on a roll."

"Hey remember back in the day when we used to kill them pigs. A couple a times, I had food in my pockets."

"Get the fuck outa here! You didn't eat on the kill floor."

They both laugh. "You a hungry motherfucker G."

"No doubt." G says.

Cleverness turns his attention to Joe and Shevonne. "These motherfuckers eat out of garbage cans so they don't care."

He shakes his head. "Now why you want to talk to me?" Cleverness asks Joe.

Joe says, "You were there when I had my revelation. You will help me find the cave of the vampire so that I may bring light."

"Cleverness looks at G and says, "You believe this shit?" Food flies from G's mouth involuntarily as he roars with laughter.

He says, "You got a lot of crazy on that couch." He continues laughing.

"I believe in you." Shevonne says, her eyes are filled with admiration and insanity.

"Say something that makes some sense or I'm throwing your ass outta here" Cleverness says.

Joe knows the importance of the next words he speaks. Joe looks right into Cleverness eyes and says, "You know something or someone that will help me do God's will. I know that you are not a believer but you must find it odd that we keep appearing in each other's lives. I am willing to do whatever it takes. I have even faced bullets to do Gods work."

"Oh shit, he's the dude!" G shouts.

He points and stands. Cleverness says, "What are you talking about?"

"Remember when we were on 125th at that meet and everybody was talking about that bank robbery."

"Yeah."

"He's the one, the one that kept coming while they were blasting at him!"

"No shit!" Cleverness responds.

G is already on the computer and they watch Joe on U-Tube. Cleverness watches, he just keeps repeating in a low voice.

"Motherfucker, Motherfucker, I can't believe it."

He keeps looking at the video and back at Joe.

Shevonne is skipping around the room and singing, "I told you, I told you."

G and Cleverness look at Joe with a new respect. The kind of respect you give someone who is not afraid to die. The telephone rings. It is Racine.

She says, "I need your help."

"You ain't call me in months and you still ain't said hello." He replies.

"Hello, Marcus, I'm sorry. Things are just crazy here."

He says, "Call me Cleverness, Rae like I told you when you were working up here."

"And like I told you when I was up there, I'm calling you the same thing Aunt Clara calls you and I don't recall her ever calling you clever." He smiles.

"Let's keep my mama outta this. What you want now?"

"I'm looking for a guy. You might have seen him on the news. He saved those two ladies in the bank robbery."

"Go ahead." He says.

"Well we had him hidden away and he wandered off. There are reports that place him in the South Bronx. We have got to get to him before some other reporters scoop him up."

"Is there a reward involved?" he asks.

"If you can find him I can get you some cash." She says.

"Like $10,000?" He asks.

"No Marcus, maybe like $500."

"I think I know where to find him If you can get it up to 2 Gs, I can have him sitting in the living room in an half hour." He says.

"Are you serious, cause if you are I can probably get the money."

"Call me when you're sure." Cleverness said.

"This is no way to treat family." Racine says as she hangs up the phone.

Noble opens the door to her office, "Any luck?"

"I got somebody working on it. He is a hustler, he is asking for $2,000. You got that kind of money?"

"Yeah, I'll pay for it and try to get it back later. You know how bad we need him."

"I'll call him back right now." Racine says.

Cleverness answers the phone "Yeah, Rae."

"I got the money, get the guy." She says.

"OK Rae but it's gonna cost you a little bit more."

"I can't get no more money Marcus, I thought we had a deal. You may have done some things I don't like but you always kept your word."

"Word is bond, you know that. I am talking about something else. My girl Shevonne, is mad sick. She had some things happen and she just lost it. They don't seem to be doing anything for her at Lincoln Hospital. You know they good at gunshot wounds, shit like that but she seems to be getting worse. You got those hook ups. I need one of them Park Ave doctors to look at her."

"Marcus I can't afford a Park Ave doctor for me but I will try to look out for you. I remember Shevonne, she was a good person dealing with a lot of stuff. Sorry to hear about that."

"Yeah, cous, you don't know half of what she's been through. Try to make that happen."

"I will do what I can but Marcus I need the guy now. Do you need a description, when will you get back to me."

"I got him right here Rae, he's sitting right here on Shevonne's couch." Joe looks up.

Racine says, "How did you – He's there. When did you –Has he been there the whole time?"

"Yes."

"But you still took us for $2,000?"

"Yeah I did, didn't I? Maybe now you will start calling me Cleverness."

She smiles and says, "You know I'm going to smack you in the head when I see you." He laughs and hangs up. Racine rushes to find Noble.

"I got him!"

Noble grabs his jacket and says, "Let's go."

Cleverness says to Joe, "You just made me some money boy."

G asks excitedly, "What's up?"

"My cousin works for SLD News. They looking for this cat and they gonna pay me some ends for finding him."

"How much did you get?" G asks.

"Let's just say you can super-size when you go to McDonalds."

"So that's my cut?" G says.

"Nothing but the best for you kid." Cleverness responds.

Cleverness turns his attention to Joe. "Why you run man?"

"I did not run. I knew it was time for me to leave. I was right, I found you." Joe says.

"I'ma ask you again, what do you want with me?"

Joe answers, "I don't know but I feel that you will guide me to the one I seek?"

"You gotta do better than that man. What you want to hang out with me for, to be my shadow, what?" G is laughing.

"I could never explain you to the people I hang with. They would think I was as crazy as.." He stops talking and looks sadly at Shevonne who is talking to herself and gesturing wildly.

"Look", Cleverness says, "You want me to help you, you want me to believe you some angel or some shit. Help my baby. You help her and I will help you." Cleverness bargains.

"I agree to your terms. " Joe says.

Joe calls Shevonne over to him. She starts crying tears of joy and drops to her knees. Joe drops too and places his hands on both of her cheeks.

"Do you believe?" He asks.

"Yes" she is trembling.

"Do you believe?" He asks again.

"Yes!" She screams and then softly repeats again and again, "Yes, yes, I believe, I do."

"Then I will drive the demons from your body, from your mind and all of your possessions. Do you know me?"

"Yes, yes." She repeats now eyes closed, quieter now like she is in a trance.

Cleverness panics, "Hey you freak get away from her." And he yanks Joe up and tosses him toward the couch. Shevonne lunges toward Joe and lands on top of him on the couch. She squeezes him and starts rocking. Joe's heart begins to beat faster and he feels nervous. There is a loud knock at the door. G and Cleverness pull their weapons and move into positions near the door. They move with the precision of a SWAT team.

G yells, "What's up?"

"It's Lenny man." "G opens the door slowly gun still out.

"What the fuck you banging on the door like the police for?"

"I didn't know y'all were up here. I wanted to make sure Shevonne would hear me. You know sometime she be sleep or in her own world."

Cleverness interrupts, "What the fuck you want Lenny?"

"There was this dude looking for you, a country boy, like Jimmy Joe Bob or some shit. Big as hell and wide, I bet he couldn't fit through this door."

Cleverness seemed excited. "When did you see him?"

"About one o clock."

"Did he say he would be back?"

"Yeah he said that if I saw you tell you to stay put. He would roll back through in two days."

Shevonne is moaning. "Oooo, Oooo".

Shevoone has a vacant and goofy look on her face as she grinds on top of Joe. Joe manages to throw her off before Cleverness reaches them. Joe is terrified and excited. Being pinned down frightened him. Then he felt stimulated and began to have a vague memory of having hurt someone when he felt this way. This is why he was terrified. Shevonne was pleased that he didn't get hard. This confirmed in her mind that he was a savior. Yes, a man that gets hard is a god who bleeds.

There is a knock at the door again this time more quietly. It is Racine and Noble. Noble scans the room for Joe and sees that he is shaken.

"What did you do to him?" He yells.

"He's ok." Cleverness responds.

Noble looks around sees the gun on the table and the hostile looks his yelling has produced. He lowers his voice.

"Joe what's wrong?"

"Do you remember Adam and Eve?" Joe says.

Confused Noble replies "Yes but what…"

"Adam and Eve and the power of the serpent." Joe is trembling and his voice sounds shaky.

"First God threw the devil out of heaven and banished him to earth where he does evil. He and God compete on earth for the minds of men. My mind had tossed out the serpent and it was heaven. Now the beast surges through my brain, it wiggles through my thoughts leaving its' slime. Descend, descend, he swallows virtue. Vertebrae by vertebrae, he uses his fangs, to go lower and lower. He drags my goodness to the lower depths where he dwells. He takes my goodness to the darkness of my loins. From there he will plot to destroy me."

"What is he talking about?" Racine asks.

"I don't know Racine, Shevonne was on top of him maybe she scared him." Noble says.

Noble looks panicked. Racine looks at Shevonne who is now grinding against the sofa. Racine grabs Noble's wrist, walks a few steps down the hall and whispers.

"It looks like he just got a little aroused and for some reason that scares him."

You need to just talk him down. Reinforce his religious side. Tell him to remember his mission and how the people need to hear what he has to say."

Noble whispers back, "You seem to know what to say why don't do it."

"Well because I think he should not be close to a woman right now. Agreed?" Noble nods.

Cleverness says, "I don't know what y'all are talking about but I need my money."

Racine responds, "I got your money, man." Noble walks over to console Joe.

"Joe I know you are going through something that I don't fully understand. I do know, however, that you are someone special sent to us at a time when we need your kind of wisdom. Freedom and justice, goodness and mercy have lost their meaning. The word freedom that gave slaves hope and kept POW's alive is now the rallying cry to invade nations.

"Churches that once served God now serve the warlike and the wealthy. The poor and the sick as despised as are the programs that would reduce their misery. They do not banish the words. They distort and pervert their meaning until they lose their power and elegance. The words are gutted and our souls are diminished. Up is down, down is up, sane is insane. We need to hear the truth from someone with no agenda, no goal of profit or fame. We need to hear you speak and we will recognize your authenticity. We need to hear your voice, honesty and sincerity. I only pray that we will remember these things when we hear them."

Joe looks around and says to Noble, "Thank you."

Shevonne is now looking at Joe and starts to move toward him. Racine is alert and intervenes.

"Shevonne, remember me?"

Shevonne looks at her intently, sizing her up. She tries to process her familiarity and frowns when she cannot remember.

Racine says, "I remember how much you liked that green purse. I saw one just like it only a little bigger."

She has Shevonne's attention how. She motions to Noble to get Joe out. Before Joe leaves, he asks Noble, "Can you get me more money?"

Noble is wealthy but is beginning to wonder how much this is all going to cost in the end.

"How much?"

"$3000."Joe says.

"Why do you need so much?" Noble asks.

"I have friends who live in the streets that I want to help and I want to give Marcus some money for his time."

"See Rae, now you got this freak calling me Marcus." Cleverness says.

G smiles and says, "A grand is a grand, money."

"What do you want?" Cleverness asks while looking at Joe.

Joe says, "I want to be with you on Wed, day and night. You must promise that no matter what is happening you must insure that we stay together. If you do this I will give $1000 and I will cure Shevonne."

Cleverness says, "Okay, I promise I will let you hang with me on Wed." Joe says.

"Wed day and night, as long as I want." Joe says.

"Yeah, yeah Wed as long as you want and I get a grand and Shevonne is cured." Cleverness says with a smirk.

"But if Shevonne is not cured you have to give me another thousand." Cleverness says looking at Noble and smiling.

"Yes." Joe says but I have another condition.

"What?" "I call you Marcus like Racine."

"Sure freak sure." Cleverness says.

Joe says, "She will be cured in 12 days."

Shevonne won't be distracted anymore. Joe tells her and Racine to come in the room with him. Shevonne again becomes entranced. He asks Racine to leave. Fifteen minutes later Joe emerges from the room with a calm Shevonne. They are all stunned.

He says, "I will give you a potion to give to her each day. Can you have someone come and get it? Racine will know where I'm staying."

"S-sure." Cleverness says still overcome by what he has witnessed.

"Good, see you soon Marcus." Joe says.

Joe, Noble and Racine leave. As the door is closing, they hear G say, "Yo first dudes shoot bullets at him point blank and don't kill him and now Shevonne-one minute she fucking the couch and now she's straight. Are we high or is this shit a miracle?"

Chapter 8

As Cleo Bloodworthy returns from Hawaii, he remembers his first flight. His father had recently returned from a business trip and was telling his mother how full the clouds looked. Cleo was astonished to find that people could ride above the clouds and begged his father to take him on his next flight. When that time came, he was very afraid. The danger of lifting off the ground so incredibly high was intense but overwhelmed by his eagerness to soar to heights unknown.

The plane continued to rise, his nerves were tingling, his body a vessel for fear and anticipation. The plane leveled off and with his nose glued to the window, he saw the fluffy white clouds of different shapes and sizes and imagined them as monsters and weird animals. He wanted to walk on them and imagined a castle deep within. He thought any minute some creature will pop its' head up and then disappear in mist.

His father was amused by Cleo's excitement. He said to him, "Cleo, all of history's richest and most powerful men, Kings, Pharaohs, Caesar all commanded huge armies, presided over great spectacles, the marvels of their time but never got to see this view. I bet they would have given almost anything to look down on their empires, to see what you see now."

At the time, it made him feel strong, more powerful than anyone. That moment for him represented youth, first time feelings, and the birth of adventure. Life was new; there was wonder everywhere.

Today he knew that like the kings who would never see the clouds below them, he would not see his youth again.

As he looks out the window, he watches Tiffany sleep. He knows her beauty and innocence is but a mask but the mask is flawless. He glances at a weak reflection of himself in the window. It lacks detail but he can see the slight sags, the lines, and the dead or dying hair, cold old gray. He is aging fast, despite keeping in shape, mountain climbing, skiing, jogging and swimming, he is land bound looking up at the clouds.

Am I a vampire? Is it in my blood? He thinks. He wonders if his aging will ever cease. He wonders could there be anything more horrible than to live eternity as an old man?

The telephone rings interrupting his thoughts. It is Congressman Moural from Nebraska. He is the Chairman of the Defense Appropriations Committee.

"Hello Cleo how was the trip."

"It's not over yet. I am still on the plane trying to soak up the last bit of leisure before we hit the ground." Cleo says.

"Oh did you want me to call back," The Congressman asks, slightly worried.

"No Adam, I am always ready to hear good news and make more money. Please continue."

Moural hesitates for a moment. "I'm afraid it's not good. It looks like we are going to have trouble with two of your projects. The new

President and Secretary of Defense are pushing hard for swifter, more portable weapons and moving away from the conventional stuff."

Bloodworthy sounds a little annoyed "Yeah but the conventional stuff, as you put it, is what you advised me to buy."

"Yes Cleo and you have made hundreds of million in profits. Look I am not saying the fight is over. I am just keeping you informed like we agreed."

"OK Adam, send me some specifics so I know how I can help you work the inside game. I will take care of the rest. Good work, say hello to Iris Marie and the kids."

"Damn." He said as he ended the call. Tiffany wakes up.

"What's up?" She asks.

"Expensive incompetence." He replies.

She waits to see if he will share the source of his frustration. Sometimes he does, sometimes he doesn't.

"I have billions invested in a couple of weapons systems and it looks like my contracts are going to be dropped."

"Why?" She asks,

"They are saying that my weapons are outdated and no longer needed. They are too slow, big and cumbersome."

"Are they?" She asks.

"Yeah, Tiffany but that's not the point. We don't need hot dogs, sodas or movie popcorn. We don't need off road vehicles, diamond bracelets or nipple rings, it's all about marketing."

"But aren't the weapons systems more important than those things."

"No TM, not from a business standpoint. It's just a product. You make customers think that they need it, you make them think yours is the best. You pay someone to advocate for it and then you influence the advocate, so that they will continue to prioritize your product."

"I understand that part but what I'm asking is if everybody in defense does the same thing, are we safe?"

He says, "We spend more on weapons than all the other countries of the world combined. Yes, we are safe, even if half of them don't work. The other half works fine and they pay us handsomely.

That's the only reason I put up with people like that crappy little congressman who just called me."

"So how do you save your weapons?" she asks.

"I do two things. I influence the men voting on the appropriations committee, I know what makes each of them happy and I know what makes them afraid. It is like poker you play the person, not the cards. The second thing I do is increase the climate of fear, so that citizens who hear about cuts in defense will cringe with terror."

"Are people so easily manipulated?" She asks.

"Are you kidding? How many people buy products just because there is a pretty woman standing near the merchandise? The ad implies woman will like you, or that it will improve your status or your power.

"Rap music is your most raw example of this. The videos show beautiful willing women, rich possessions and the words they use are words of power. That is all most of us want."

"What about morality, culture, religion?" she asks.

"Do you know anyone who is truly moral who is not also afraid? Yes, there are Ghandis, Mandelas and Kings but most people are moral because they fear the consequences of being immoral, not because it is right. Given the option, they would choose to ravage women and humble their enemies.

"Culture is fine but low on the hierarchy of needs. It is need, not culture that drives us, that compels us. As for religion, it is the greatest cause of war, the opiate of the masses, and in most of the world robs more money than banks or taxes." She asks, "What do you believe in besides a world of power, sex and riches?" "I believe in many things but I know that if I want to sell products to people, I must understand them."

"I think that if you are right, that is very sad." she says.

"No need to cry. These needs in the hands of imaginative men have produced wealth, which led to leisure time to create the arts. Man's existence was once subsistence and survival. It is wealth that gave us the leisure time to appreciate beauty in nature and then to create it ourselves."

"Is there anything intrinsically good? She asks. He thought for a moment.

"Babies, perhaps" He said. The plane lands and they head for home.

The head of Wolf News is watching Noble interview J.C. Doe. He again is calling his producers. Each time he is angrier.

"Why the fuck don't we have this guy. There is no such thing as an exclusive anymore!"

"We can't find him to offer him a deal. He was seen in the Bronx but he disappeared."

"Get some pros on this. Get investigators to find him and research to find out who he is. I want to know all about this guy, his family, where he works, if he has any dirt and no more fucking excuses!"

Carl Goldstream continued to watch Noble's interview feeling deeply frustrated.

"So Joe we have received more calls, e-mails and twitters after your first two interviews than when Michael Jackson died. How does that make you feel."

"I am humbled by the response."

"We have a lot of questions that came in for you that have nothing to do with the bank robbery. Do you mind answering?" He shrugs.

"Okay, okay Mike from Connecticut wants to know "Who is the person you most admire?""

"There are so many people now and throughout history that deserve mention that I would do a disservice to too many people if I were to name just one but all of these people have things in common. They love justice. They pray for peace. They give. They seek wisdom. They worship truth. They have faith and vision. They are moral and kind. They are brave and they are rare. They are God's will."

Joe's answer inspires Nobel. He realizes that Joe is like some great actor who is extraordinary as a person and when he takes the stage, is magical. Joe's words resonate, his eyes mesmerize and his energy embraces.

"Do you mean they are doing God's will?"

"No I mean they are Gods will or that his force dominates their actions and existence. It is like flight for a bird, the bird may land and even kill its food but it is primarily a thing that flies. These men and women have flaws, they have bad moments but their essence is love of others. They are not judgmental and they are forgiving. They do not feel the need to criticize others and they feel empathy. They see their own faults and seek enlightenment."

"What about sin?" Noble asks.

"I am saying that we should work on our own sins. I am saying that we all sin and God is our judge. If I focus on the sins of someone who is different from me, I am simply expressing my hatred and suspicion of those different from me and using religion to do that.

"If I believe in a religion that loves the poor and helps the sick then I cannot be against spending my taxes to help the sick and feed the poor. What we have now is in many of our biggest churches is a religion that serves the rich, appeals to our worst instincts and appears to have our lords consent, even his blessing. The result is guilt-free sin. The salvation that these poor souls seek, their spiritual growth is stunted by preachers that teach that their flaws are flight."

After a few more questions, he thanks Joe and ends the interview. The twitters and e-mails arrive at a furious pace. Joe is a star, a superstar and Noble has him. Newspapers are running features about him; he is the talk at the water cooler and on Facebook. Rival news organizations are drooling and planning. They want their own interview. Even competitors at SLD are demanding that he appear on their show.

Noble has a plan in place to get Joe away from the station to some secluded location. He even has two decoy cars and men dressed like Joe. He can manage that but he knows he has to face his greatest fear. He knows he will have to uncover Joe's past and he does not know where that will lead .He knows he must because with a story of this magnitude, others will be looking for dirt and without knowing the truth he could place the SLD and himself in a dangerous position.

A few days later and after much thought he decided to let Christie handle things. She is the best researcher he knows. She is the only non-reporter in the Le Plume group. She is gifted and tenacious.

"Christie, it's Noble I .."

"Let me guess, you need information on your guy, Joe Doe. I am doing research for three other clients. Everyone wants to know Joe."

"I know this is a lot to ask Christie but can you give it to me first, so that I know what's coming." Christie thought for a moment.

"OK I will give you a few days but it will cost you a favor and heavy cash."

"OK thanks Christie." Noble was relieved. "What you got so far."

"$10,000?" Christie says,

"Jesus Christie!"

"Noble I'm going easy on you because you're a friend. You know there are magazines that would give me $25,000 to break this first."

Noble thought about it. SLD would probably pay half of expenses. He said to Christie "Bill me $20,000 and I'll get them to pay half. The cheap bastards will gripe but they will pay $10,000 if they think I have to pay it too."

Noble is anxious. "Okay, what you got?"

"First you can stop calling him Joe. His name is Adam Robeson. His friends call him Ellis. That is his middle name. His father was a steelworker from Pennsylvania. Although small in stature, he was one of the company's most reliable workers.

"Despite the drudgery of the job and the life draining heat, he had a pleasant disposition and was always happy to see his family. The pay was good and he did not live extravagantly. He took pride in being able to afford nice vacations for the family every year. His mother was from Minnesota and seemed to her friends to be excessively happy with life's routines. She taught elementary school, conducted food drives for the poor and held private art lessons for a small fee.

"She loved classical music and had her husband install speakers all over the house, including the bathroom. Their names, by the way were Jonathan and Marie." Noble listened, pleased by the detail of her research but he was eager to learn more about Joe. She continued.

"Everything seemed to be going fine in their life until the plant started laying off people. His father's deterioration was slow. At first, he insisted nothing would change. Marie continued to spend at the same rate and go about her activities. Jonathan, always stoic, began to communicate less and less. Each day he left to look for work, competing with hundreds of other men who had suddenly lost their job.

"One day he arrived home late, he had to walk five miles because he ran out of gas. He went into the garage, picked up a gas can, walked out and never came back. Marie and young Ellis moved from city to city. She began to live life in her head, longing for better days. Eventually she began having extended conversations and social teas with imagined guests. She began to ignore Ellis. He quickly had to become provider and parent."

Racine bursts in to Noble's office. "Noble you got to come right away."

He could see the urgency on Racine's face. "Noble come on." She repeats.

Noble is still transfixed by Joe's story. Racine becomes more insistent and grabs Noble by the arm. Noble stands while yelling to Christie "I'll call you right back, don't go anywhere."

He turns to Racine annoyed and yanking his arm back "What is it, Racine. I was getting Joe's story. What's so damn important?"

"Joe has accepted invitations to speak at 10 churches. He will speak at Riverside Church and St. Patrick's Cathedral on Sunday. Both churches cancelled scheduled speakers at the request of their members."

"How did they get in touch with him?" he asks.

"Apparently he got in touch with them. Remember Lenny from my cousin's house. I think he is working for Joe now. He saw Joe cure Shevonne and had some kind of awakening. He says he is devoted to Joe now and follows him around doing whatever he asks."

"How did you find out about this?"

"St. Patrick's called up to finalize some details with Joe. You were on the phone so someone here gave the call to me."

Noble says, "We can't let him speak to them, we don't know what he will say and with a public appearance, we won't be exclusive anymore. We cannot lose control of this already. Maybe we can talk him out of this."

Racine saw the fear of loss in Cronkite's eyes and tried to be as consoling as she could.

"Cronk, you knew this couldn't last." She took his hand. "You did a great job keeping him exclusive for this long. We can't keep him prisoner. He seems like a loyal guy and if we don't mess up this relationship by trying to bully him, we still have the inside track." He looks at her sadly and knowingly nods. Racine says, "You know Noble, I think it's time we brought in the others from Le Plume. I think Joe is still the best way we have of making news matter again. This may be our last opportunity to save what we love and Joe is our savior."

"Hey Noble you got a call." Someone yells.

"Take a message." Noble responds.

"It's the Joe Doe guy." They both pause and then hurry toward the phone.

"Hello Joe where are you?"

"I am downstairs, I want to come up."

"I will send someone down to get you. Should I order something for you to eat?"

"No but I want to see my mail."

"Got it, I will see you in my office."

Noble sent someone to get Joe, he did not want him standing around outside. He knew rival news groups were looking for him. Noble and Racine walked back to the office, and before she could even ask, Noble said, "He wants to see his mail."

"Why?" she said.

"I guess we will find out in a minute."

Joe walks in. He looks a lot different from when Noble met him for the first time. He is neater and the beard is not scraggly. He is not as thin. He has gained a slight bit of muscle and is wearing new clothes. Yet his gaze is still as magnetic and his presence as distinct. He has an aura of great humility and great power. He is like the last of a once great species facing extinction.

Joe smiles and bows slightly and then continues his effortless gait. "Hello Racine, how good to see you and Noble how are you?"

They return the greeting and after some polite conversation, Racine says, "Cronk here tells me you want to see the mail."

"Yes I was looking at the television and the reporter read e-mails from people. Some were very strange and others asked for help or advice. I wanted to see if I could be of service."

"I understand', Noble replied, "but you have received letters in the tens of thousands, hundreds of thousands if you include e-mail. Obviously you can't read it all, how do you want to attack it?"

"Well I will feel my way through it. I sometimes get strong feeling about things. Today the Lord spoke to me as I was watching the e-mails."

Racine felt alarmed but didn't show it.

"Is this the first time God has spoken to you through the TV?"

Joe concentrates, then responds "I have been homeless so I don't remember watching TV."

"Do you remember anything about your past?" She asks.

Noble tries to get Racine's attention. He does not want to have this conversation until he knows learns more about Joe's past from Christie.

"Ahh Joe, you don't have to talk about this now. Let's see if I can get the mail for you." Racine looks at Noble, surprised by his interruption. Joe responds.

"Its fine, I don't mind. As I said, I don't remember much. It is just quick flashes of images, out of sequence. Sometimes I feel sad or scared. Sometimes I am just am observer, engaged and anxious, like watching a horror movie. I feel fear but I want to know how it ends."

Racine watches Joe leave with Noble. He is blind. He does not see that this thing may blow up in his face. All he can see is the story; He is important again, he is relevant. Racine thinks only of the resurrection of real news. She is disappointed. Joe was the person she hoped would be media's savior. She now realizes that Joe may be a Paranoid Schizophrenic.

Noble has selected an office for Joe. The computer at the desk is set so that he can view his e-mail. Joe asks to be left alone and Noble leaves. Once alone, he puts one hand on the computer and one hand on the stacks of envelopes and begins his prayer.

"Dear father, it is I your child, your servant and the embodiment of your will. I pray that you will send the eternal force, in abundance and let it radiate through the walls of ignorance. The people must know truth. They must love another and crave virtue. I beg you to let me guide humankind to that which has been lost. I pray for your protection as I journey to the cave of the Vampire. I pray to you, father, the essence of all that is good."

Chapter 9

Carl Goldstream listened quietly as Cleo chewed him out. "I want this guy stopped in his tracks. Do you know what he represents?"

"Yes he means big numbers, SLD's ratings sky rocket every time his segment airs."

"No, no I mean yes we need to get him for the ratings but he is destructive. He is trying to resurrect a Jesus that we have long since killed. He is the opposite of the neo-Christ we have marketed. He must be repositioned as evil, as liberal. We must kill the message by muddying the messenger. You know the drill. I want something on this guy and I want it now!"

Goldstream is trying to think of a way to reassure Bloodworthy when he sees something on his monitor.

"Wait Mr. Bloodworthy", Goldstream says before Cleo hangs up. "I'm getting something now. It looks like he will be appearing at Riverside Church and St. Patrick's this Sunday. It looks like SLD is going live and I think the other networks will follow."

"Damn, I wanted more time to create this guy." Cleo says,

"OK let's start with the questions. 'Who is this guy?' Use the poverty thing 'Could he be a communist?" 'Was he in on the bank robbery?

"I want all our headliners to lead with this. Get our groups yelling about it and get our experts on the other networks to work these questions into as many of the other news shows as possible; Get anything that we can go negative with. Got it?"

"Yes sir."

Goldstream intensified his use of threats and rewards to get information on Joe. He called their detective service and they had nothing new. He called one of the anchors. The anchors were the highest paid employees at other news stations. At Wolf, they were more like the intro act for their opinion celebrities masquerading as newsmen.

"Hey Rob, I need you to work in a few negative questions about that guy from the robbery. Something like' Witnesses said that the guy said he was Jesus.' Then run some footage of the Jonestown massacre and show a couple of stills of Charlie Manson. Say that people have been asking if he the head of a cult."

"Ok." Rob replies and before he can say anything else, Goldstream has moved on to the next call.

"Hello Beck, Carl Goldstream here."

"Hello Carl what you got?"

"Beck, Rob is going to mention that Joe, you know the guy from the robbery, may be a cultist. I want you to mention that on you show using Wolf News as the source."

"Sounds good boss, I can also say that no one knows where this guy comes from. I can ask, 'Is he a terrorist?'"

"Yes, yes that sounds really good. Let's go with that."

"I'm on it." Lowbrow says as Goldstream ends the call.

His next call is to his chief editor at the Extreme Daily, Reversal's largest newspaper.

"I want some anger generated about the cost of this guy Joe's appearance at Riverside Church. 'Is it a real Christian church?' Talk about the radicals that have spoken there. 'Why is he going to Harlem?

"For St. Patrick's let's find some irate Catholics that don't want this false prophet at their church. I am also going to get this going on our talk radio shows. By six pm all the cable stations will be asking the same questions with their idiotic pro and con format."

"Yes sir." The editor responds. Now for the icing on the cake Goldstream thinks. He has one of his people call Perfectly United Kinship of Evangelist, the grass-root conservative organization sponsored by Reversal.

If they can get ten people out there, Wolf will cover them and accuse the other media of being leftist if they do not. Goldstream calls Cleo to let him know the work is done. Bloodworthy grins and says to Goldstream.

"He thinks he is a hero coming to his coronation, by Sunday he will be a leper arriving at his lynching." Bloodworthy continues planning in the darkness of his room.

Joe has completed reading the letters and e-mails. He has responded to hundreds of the letters and more people have begged to become followers of Joe. They have offered to serve him unconditionally for proximity to him and for spiritual guidance. Others have sent envelopes with checks or cash. He has many offers to speak and women have made a range of offers from sexual adventure to marriage.

Joe has gathered his seven new followers, including Lenny in a room.

"I want all of you to truly know each other. I want you to be brothers in spirit as loyal to each other as you are to me. So I ask you to tell your stories, tell the reason you are here today. Lenny would you mind beginning?"

Lenny is now dressed in a white robe, dress pants and sandals like Joe. "Is there anything special you want me to talk about?" Lenny asks.

"Tell what is in your heart." Joe says.

"I am twenty -two years old or I will be in two weeks. My life was pretty good, you know the normal shit. Oh excuse me Server."

"It is ok, try not to do say that word. You're fine Lenny, please continue."

"Yes Server."

Joe had asked that the others call him Server to remind them that we are all here to serve one another but also to express humility as their leader.

Lenny continued, "I was saying that I have not been right since I was thirteen. I walked up on these four guys about 30 or 35 you know and they was raping my sister's friend. She was only about eleven years old and really sweet man. You know like innocent. She was a couple of years younger than me and in my sister's class.

"They were all in an alley and I can remember the smell. At first like regular garbage and then like some dead shit, you know. One guy was beating her in the ribs and the other two well one was in her mouth and her panties were down. I didn't even realize I was walking toward them until the fourth guy grabbed me.

"He was the lookout I guess or he just liked watching. I was about to shout, 'Leave her alone!' when he backhanded me across the face. It hurt like nothing I had ever felt and still until today y'all, I don't think I ever been hit that hard. He told me to leave and not say anything or they would do the same thing to me. I was beginning to focus again after the smack and I saw her eyes man." Lenny begins to tear up.

"She had this look of sheer terror I mean like fear to the depth of her soul man and then blank, nothing there, nothing. It was like I watched her soul leave her body. I had never seen anything so sad. I stumbled out of the alley. My nose and lip were bleeding. I saw a cop car down the street and I ran yelling, 'Help, help.' I took them to the alley and the cops yelled 'Freeze.' They shot and hit two guys and they dropped. One guy hopped up on a garbage can to a fence and over. The last guy held on to her and used her as a shield. He held her up, took out his gun, shot, and hit one of the cops. They backed away and he jetted. He left the girl in a dumpster. She was barely alive. Forty - five days later, it is my birthday.

"It was Saturday morning and I raced out of my room to take a look at my presents. Instead, what I saw was my mom and pops bound and gagged in the living room. They had beaten my dad unconscious and my mom was crying and begging them with her eyes to leave me alone. It was the same guy who slapped me in the alley. He hit me and knocked me out.

"I woke up lying flat on my back in the dark. I tried to sit up and bumped my head. It hurt and I was almost unconscious again. I slumped back down. I was about to raise my hands to see what I bumped into and felt something in my hand. It was a lighter; you know one of them two for a dollar kind. I flicked it, the flame was low but I could see I was in some kind of big white box.

"I moved the light around and saw that my birthday cake was in there. I started to light the candles for more light but I saw the shadow of red and brown circles near my leg at the bottom of the box. I moved my feet trying to kick whatever it was closer to me so I could see with the lighter. Once I got the circles close to me I put the lighter near them and leaned forward."

Lenny was crying now. He wiped away tears and paused to collect himself.

"It was my mom and dad's heads and their hands. Their eyes were open and blank just like the girl in the alley. I started screaming and hitting the top of the box. I was kicking the inside of the box and my mother's head rolled over my face. I started trembling and I had my first seizure." Lenny pauses again.

"When I woke up I could hear them digging me up. The cops had shot the guy that hit me and the other guy confessed. I was in a refrigerator. When they pulled me out, I was holding on to my parents hands. I wouldn't let go. I was covered in dried blood and cake. They said I only had about an hour of air left.

When I saw Server save those ladies from the bank, I wished he had been there to save the girl." He said more quietly "and to save me."

Then at the house, I saw him save Shevonne. She was beyond crazy. I saw him save her and I knew if I had any chance of my life being right again it would be through him."

Lenny was still shedding tears and trying to wipe them away in the most manly and least noticeable way. Joe embraced him and said something that made Lenny smile momentarily. He asked Lenny if he wanted he leave the room. Lenny returned in five minutes ready to hear the next Servant of the Server.

His name was Terry Stiles. He was a captain in Special Forces.

"I joined the Army after 911. I wanted to go to Afghanistan but they sent me to Iraq. I joined at age 25. I was into martial arts, boxing at the gym four times a week.

"Before enlisting, I had three girlfriends and was on the lookout for the next opportunity. I owned a small restaurant next to one of these upscale spas and ladies were always popping in and flirting. I was doing good, going out to their houses in the Hamptons, swimming in their pools. I had some cash and I was in demand."

Stiles manages a little smile which quickly fades.

"When the world trade, when the towers got hit, I was downtown at this Greek restaurant with this attorney, she worked for a bank that had its' headquarters there. She was this redhead with so much energy, like she didn't want to miss a minute of life and she lived it at full blast. We had shared a huge salad and some wine.

She said she had to make a stop and …"Stiles pauses, "We took the subway down to the towers. It was a little windy but I sat outside. I saw the first plane hit. The ground shook like an earthquake. I saw the fire and the dozens of people leaping from the building. I saw those on the window ledge deciding whether their lives would end in flame or shattered and contorted on the sidewalk below. People were scared on the ground, traffic was stopped, and people ran away or stared in horror and disbelief. I tried to reach her by phone remembering she was in the second building.

"I could barely hear her. She said people were stampeding, trying to get to the elevator and stairways. I guess the phone got knocked out of her hand. I could hear the voices, the chaos and the desperation. I kept looking at the building hoping she would come out. Then I heard that eerie sound, the engine noise piercing through the air as the second plane hit. The phone fell silent and thousands died as I watched helplessly.

"I sold the restaurant and joined the Army. My life had one purpose-to kill the enemy. I was good at killing and led my men to many victories. I made sure they were well trained, motivated and focused. Still I could not stop our guys from being blown up by IED's.

"Walking along the roads or driving in trucks, we were fair game for these homemade bombs. This fueled my homicidal impulses. My patriotism, my honorable sacrifice was becoming simple blood lust. When you kill enough people either you never care about killing again or you get enough and you need to restore your balance.

"When my tour finished I started an organization of vets to protect our troops. We weren't getting enough help from the government and it seemed that guys that had never served were getting rich and vets were homeless. We had guys from intelligence and computer guys, so we started following the money." He shakes his head.

"Everybody was getting rich, billions of dollars in contracts for gas, for meals in Iraq. They ripped off taxpayers and under-served soldiers. They charged for rebuilding that never happened. They flew in 12 billion in cash loaded on pallets and claimed to have given it out to Iraqi officials to run the government but there was no evidence. Not one receipt. They were robbers and thieves who used 911 to deflect any criticism or suspicion about what they were doing. They betrayed us and stole from us. They made us human sacrifices for their war profiteering. I became so disillusioned that I was no longer able to trust. I began to feel that everything was fake, everything was a con until I saw the Server on television. He is authentic; I felt him immediately. I dedicate myself to him."

As the next Servant was about to speak Shevonne entered the room. Lenny said, "Hey Shevonne, what are you doing here?"

She said, "I want to be like you, I want to serve Joe." She turns to Joe.

"Joe you healed me, you saved my life. I want to help you help other people too."

"God knows there are so many people that could use your help." Joe responds, "I am called Server now."

Joe is nervous and almost afraid to look at Shevonne. She stirs intense feelings in his head and in his belly. She scares him in a way that he does not understand. She is clean now and her outer beauty is restored. Her madness is submerged but pulsates beneath the surface.

She clings desperately to normalcy, abandoning any ambition to be the extraordinary, vibrant being she was meant to be.

"I could give out flyers, maybe clean up around here." She says looking around.

Server asks, "Shevonne does Marcus, uh Cleverness know you are here?"

"Yes, I called him and told him I would come to see you. He knows that I admire and love you. I think it bothers him."

"How do you know?" Joe asks.

"I can tell, I am a woman."

"Is he coming to Riverside Church on Sunday?"

"No he is working on some business with a special client."

"What do you mean?" Server asks.

"Cleverness drops everything whenever this guy calls. He always says that he makes the most money when he works for him. He says he gets enough money to pay bills and to make plans."

"What does Cleverness do?" Server asks.

"Whatever makes money, hustle, con, sell, buy, promote or destroy. He even came up with one of those, buy this product for $19.99 schemes on tv. We used to watch the commercials at three o'clock in the morning sometime."

"Does he sell drugs?"

"No everything but that. He respects the profit but he believes you don't do what you see everybody else doing. He says that the little things he does there are no mandatory sentences for and for the big things he gets help with from his contact."

"Tell him he is to see me on Wednesday as he promised."

"OK Joe, I mean Server, see I learn quick. What can I do?"

"I want you to be in charge of getting e-mail addresses and telephone numbers of people willing to assist our cause. I want thousands of pages of names and addresses from people in the crowd. We will need many faithful Servants to do our work."

Chapter 10

The Servant is due to arrive at Riverside Church. A large and enthusiastic awaits him. The people are lively and boisterous. There are vendors on the outskirts of the crowd selling warm food, mittens and music. Late arrivers try to jostle their way to the front, angling their bodies and stretching their necks, they move purposefully.

The children move more quickly, darting through the forest of adults. They peer through the gaps, moving forward, for them the adventure has already begun. Police and police barricades prevent the crowd from disturbing the invited guests and parishioners.

As the parishioners walk to church, most ignore the crowd and the large speakers at the top of the steps. As they watch the latecomers hurry inside, someone in the crowd begins to lead Christmas songs. A fainter competing chorus of "No justice, no peace" rivals the singing of Nat Cole's Christmas Song. Almost unnoticed and on foot, Server arrives. The Servants surround him as he quietly walks toward the entrance. People in the crowd now begin to point and yell, "It's him." Some are not sure. They are used to their heroes arriving in limos or with loud, flashing police escorts. A slow clap builds with the realization that it might be him. He stops briefly and waves toward them. People now begin to jump up and down; they lift the signs they have brought with them. Fathers place their children on their shoulders. Camera phones held high form a modern salute.

Shevonne leads volunteers into the crowd to get names and numbers. The Servant smiles and disappears behind the large doors, which now quietly close. As the minister finishes his sermon, anticipation swells. The Servant takes the stage and begins to speak.

"Good morning fellow children of a loving and all-knowing God. I greet you in the name of our father who loves us. In gratitude for the wonderful gift of life, I give my love to him and to my brothers and sisters in life, all of you. I greet you today to remind you of God's will and the shining example of prophets. Let us not be misled by the sleight of hand of satin's magicians. I remind you, it is better to give than to receive. War is not peace, hate is not Christian and judgment not yours. I know that to the good Christian and to true followers of any religion these principles are understood and practiced. It is only when wolf in sheep's clothing rise to lead the church does it promote anger and hate, greed and selfishness and do so in God's name. They bless our worst instincts; they sanctify sin.

"You will know a wolf in sheep's clothing because he will create a Christ that encourages you to hate, to hate Gays, immigrants, Blacks, liberals and poor people. To hate those who want to clean our water and air, work for a decent wage and for medicine for those who don't have it. They would have you cheer for war, capital punishment, excessive greed and intolerance. This is not holy.

"Some of you embrace these distorted teachings because it is easy. It is easier to hate someone who is different. It is easier to love our wealth than to feel the suffering of the world's poor. It is easier to claim the selfish aims of government as those of God rather than see your sin and ask God for forgiveness. You must abandon the easy path. Like the flower that emerges from the harsh earth and cold winter to the beauty of the sun, your effort will bring you a true religious experience and closer to the God you seek.

"You are told as a Christian that you must choose sides. You are on the left or on the right. There is only good and evil. You are lost because you are choosing a direction rather than a purpose. The path to love is giving and service, the path to goodness requires the courage to live a remarkable life, a life of virtue lived in loving disposition.

"This is difficult I know. You are told that you do not need to grow. You are in the best country practicing the best religion. You are told that anyone who wants to improve the country is unpatriotic and anyone one who challenges the direction of the church seeks to destroy it. I would remind you that all the great prophets challenged the existing order. They were men and women of vision, men and woman who knew their spiritual longings were unfulfilled.

"Today the devil's minions have televisions and satellites to beam his lies into the heart and minds of billions across the globe. The truth is whispered from deep inside you and struggles valiantly to be heard.

"The devil controls the wealth, the message and the weapons. He convinces you to buy more things, satisfying his need for power but you remain unfulfilled. He convinces you that you should be in a perpetual state of lust, using sex to sell his products. He creates a climate of fear and division so that you are constantly afraid or in need. You can never be happy like this.

"If we will be happy we must abandon lies, no matter where they come from. We must have new heroes. Our soldiers who fought against Hitler's evil were brave and saved humankind from untold horrors. The soldiers that fought the Revolutionary War gave birth to our nation and to remarkable principles. But if soldiers are a nation's only heroes then a society becomes militaristic.

"We need to create more heroes. We need to show admiration to great teachers and the society will become smarter. Admire great journalist and the society will become more just. Admire great philanthropist and the society becomes more giving. Admire truth-seekers and the society has more virtue.

"As was done before by those before me, I offer you my message, my time on earth, my life as your servant. You are all vessels. God knows your potential, your hearts longing. He is there within you, asking you to expel the gaudy filth that you have allowed in your temple so that he can fill you with the light of his love. The life you were meant to live awaits you."

Inside the church, people are deeply moved. Having witnessed his presence, not just his words they are more solemn and reflective. They have felt an awakening within. They sit holding hands, eyes closed.

Outside the crowd roars its approval. They chant, "Server, he's the one. No one else can get it done."

Others embrace; several young women cry tears of joy. Some raise clenched fists in support of his ideas. Reporters jostle, trying to position themselves for an interview as the Server exits. Cameramen vie for just the right angle for the perfect shot.

Racine and Noble know well the chaos that is to ensue. They have arranged to leave with the Servants who will surround a Joe look-a-like. Joe will change clothes and leave with a group of parishioners, unnoticed. They will meet later.

Cleo Bloodworthy feels energized after his vacation. He hits the gym and works out. He is in great shape for a man of his age but still keenly aware than he is not the man he was 20 years ago. He tires more quickly, he lifts less and recuperates more slowly. He asks himself, what good is his money, the power and the perks if none of it can stop the deterioration of aging. He feels age draining his life, moment by moment, slowly, deliberately, certainly, death will consume him. He wipes away the sweat with a towel. He showers and gets dressed awaiting his two o'clock appointment. He paces anxiously. He gets a call from downstairs, his guest have arrived.

"Hello sir."

Brady enters the room. He is a mercenary and long-time associate of Bloodworthy. He has fought in thirteen wars and led small groups of mercenaries and thousands of soldiers. He is a killer and who has killed men all over the world. He trained Cleo's security forces and has been contracted to 'alter circumstances' for Cleo when the need arose.

Cleo loves adventure and craves blood so on two occasions he asked to accompany Brady on dangerous missions as though booking a pleasure cruise. Brady admired Cleo. He liked that Cleo was not just another fat cat. Cleo was willing to risk his wealth and his life for that electrifying surge of adrenaline and power. Brady knows it well.

Cleo liked Brady because he reminded him of his brother, yet he was still a whole person, unbowed and unbroken by war. Cleo also liked the blood, the crack of bones split open by bullets, the smell of smoking flesh. He loved seeing life leave the bodies of soldiers who died in combat. He looked deep into the men's eyes hoping to see where life goes before it leaves a man empty.

Brady and Cleo had discussed life and death for days there in the desert. Once while passing a bottle of scotch, Brady told him the legend of the Anyman. He was reputed to be a direct descendant of the African tribe that came to Siberia. It is from this tribe that all other human types spawned. Indians, Asians and Whites were all genetic offspring from this particular group of wanderers. The blood from the people of this tribe gives vitality, energy and youth to those who drink it. For this reason, they were hunted for centuries and lived in isolation in three areas of the world. In ancient Egypt, they lived in splendor serving Pharaohs until the invasion of the Assyrians.

They second group moved to Poland and killed in Hitler's gas chambers during World War 2. The largest remaining group hides in the rain forest of Brazil. Their leader is the Anyman. He is renowned for his mystical powers and ancient wisdom. Brady found him and persuaded him to see Cleo. He has brought with him two young women who are beautiful, innocent and frightened.

Cleo eyes devour them. He wants to drain them of their blood and their innocence.

"Please come in and have a seat." Cleo says forcing his attention to the tall, thin bearded man.

The Anyman nods and sits on the floor in Bloodworthy's huge office. Cleo has noticed the spring in his step, the effortless motion. It seems as though there is a field of energy around him and he is subtly vibrating. The women hold hands and sit in a corner of the room, their soft eyes downcast.

Cleo says, "I am glad you could come and meet with me today."

The Anyman looks at Brady and says, "Your friend is very convincing."

"Yes, he can be persuasive." Cleo smiles slightly without looking at Brady.

"What shall I call you?"

"What you call me is unimportant. Just know that I am your ancestor, an ancient father from your distant past. This I can say to any man I meet because you all share my blood."

Bloodworthy is excited. He is like a wine collector who has discovered the world's most rare bottle. He cannot wait to taste the girls. He cannot wait to have the surge of new life flowing through his veins.

"So how do we do this?"

"You give me ten million dollars and I give you the girls."

Cleo thinks about bargaining, it is a reflex. Instead he replies, "Okay but I must taste; I must know what I am getting."

Anyman nods at the girls. They rise together and walk to Cleo. They stare deeply at each other, almost in a trance and then kiss each other passionately.

The taller girl holds the others head with both hands and bites her lip. The shorter girl, with her lip pouring blood kisses Cleo. He voraciously sucks her open wound. Bloodworthy instantly feels a tingling throughout his body, which quickly intensifies. He feels a pain in his chest and thinks he is going to have a heart attack. The pain then moves to his head and he has already shit in his expensive trousers.

Brady gets up and points his gun at Anyman. Anyman yells to the shorter girl in his language and the girl wrestles away from Cleo. Cleo is gasping for air and holding his chest.

"Do something!" Brady yells.

"There must be something wrong with his blood. Does he have any diseases?" Anyman asks.

Cleo is now unconscious. Brady gives Cleo CPR. Cleo awakens to Brady's mouth on his and pants full of shit. He pushes Brady away from him and looks harshly at Anyman.

He moves on unsteady legs towards the bathroom and yells, "This is bullshit."

Cleo enters the bathroom. He heads right for the toilet. He sits and removes his stained trousers and briefs and shits long, multi-colored turds. His head is beginning to clear. He feels like he is moving from a bad hangover to good high. No matter, he is going to make this guy feel pain, he thinks. He uses his phone to tell his assistant to bring him clean clothes. It seems like the shitting has ended. Finally, he thinks. He heads for the shower to clean off the mess. He cleans his body and it seems a little tighter, leaner. He shampoos and his hair feels thicker.

He wipes off quickly and looks in the mirror. He looks five years younger. The differences are subtle but they are clear to him. It is working. He feels euphoric. He puts on his robe and races into the room, his hair still wet.

"I'll pay what you ask." He quickly writes a check and hands it to Anyman.

Before he takes it, Anyman says, "You have seen the power of blood. These are two virgins from a powerful bloodline. There is no more powerful tonic save that of the blood of prophets or angels."

Cleo thanks him and says, "How young will I be? Will I be able to cheat death?"

Anyman replies, "Your body will be pain- free, your mind will be clear and you will look ten to twenty years below your age but you will die, my friend."

Cleo's euphoria turns to sadness and then to rage. He yells and grabs Anyman with both hands.

"I want to live forever. You fuckin tell me how to live forever!" Anyman is surprisingly strong and has barely moved as a result of Cleo's charge.

Still Cleo's face is inches from his when he replies, "You must be the child or the grandchild of a vampire or be bitten three times by one. If not, you must drink the blood of an angel or a living prophet."

"I know I have the blood of vampires in me." Cleo says."

Anyman says, "That could be the reason for such a strong reaction to pure human blood."

Anyman thought for a moment and then said, "But if you have less than half vampire blood you feel the thirst for human blood but it is distorted. You want to overpower humans, you despise them as lower forms but you are still one of them."

Bloodworthy, still clinging to Anyman, cries out desperately. "You must tell me what to do. Tell me now."

Anyman removes Cleo's hands forcibly and says, "You have been given an extraordinary life. You have the wealth of a small nation and the power of a king. I have brought to you the fountain of youth and two beautiful virgins. You should be overwhelmed with joy. That you are not makes me believe that if you had eternal life you would be eternally unhappy. What you need I cannot give you." Anyman's words resonate throughout the room. The girls and Brady look at Bloodworthy, awaiting his understanding but instead he responds,

"You don't know what is like not to achieve your birthright, not to live your destiny, to try everything and not quench your thirst. Most men would be happy with a large house, a fast car and a pretty girl. They are insects who have no ambition; they want softness and pleasure. They are weak and they make men like me rich. I want that which most men perceive as unattainable and I have earned these things because of my id, my unrestrained will. I have been and remain unwilling to accept the idea that anything can be denied me. It is precisely why I have you here today. I will not stop; I will not be limited, not even by death."

His assistant arrives in his office. "Your clothes are on the bed sir."

"Thank you." He says. "Brady, I will see you again soon. You have done a great job here my friend."

He pats him on the shoulder and hands him a thick envelope. Brady takes it and nods. Bloodworthy realizes what a valuable resource Anyman is, apologizes to him and gives him an extra fifty thousand. Anyman smiles and follows Brady to the door. He tells his assistant to make arrangements for the girls. They will live in a lavish cabin in upstate New York. Cleo is imagining the things he will do with them. They are beautiful and completely submissive. Maybe Tiffany will shop for negligees for them and choreograph their sexual adventures. Yes, that will be nice, he thinks. They bow and smile timidly as they leave the room. His body continues to feel light and vibrant. He is sure he can fly.

Chapter 11

The Server has completed his appearance at St. Patrick's. There are small protests against his appearance but a large and receptive crowd overwhelms them. Wolf news and most media give equal time to the 50 anti-Server protesters as they do the 30,000 people who pack the streets surrounding St. Patrick's Cathedral to cheer him. Noble and Racine again employ clever tactics to obscure Server's exit.

Shevonne has done an excellent job of collecting names and contact information. They have also handed out leaflets with the next event. So Shevonne is in a great mood when she goes to the Dr. Cogney's office. Racine arranged the doctor's visit and his office is located at a Park Ave address as Cleverness insisted. Shevonne did not want to go and would not have stayed except that the Server insisted. She felt a little intimidated and certainly looked out of place in the lavish outer office. The receptionist was very polite, however, and welcomed her to have coffee, juice or hors devours while she waited.

"The doctor is running a little late. Are you scheduled for the 11 am group?"

"Yes" Shevonne replies. "I saw him once for an individual visit. This will be my first group."

The receptionist says, "I apologize, I tried to reach you. There are six people in the group. I reached everyone but you and one other... Oh there she is now."

"Hi, I was just explaining that I was unable to reach you. He is running about 30 minutes late." The woman nods and sits.

She has large, dark shades on and a wide hat, she looks like a movie star trying to avoid the public and paparazzi. She immediately picks up a magazine, takes off her hat, releasing her long flowing hair.

She tilts her sunglasses up just over her forehead and becomes immediately engrossed in her reading. She has taken a seat as far away from Shevonne as seating will allow and has not made any eye contact with either Shevonne or the receptionist. Shevonne ignores all her avoidant body language and talks to her.

"Is this your first time?" The woman does not respond.

Shevonne moves closer to her and asks again "Is this your first time here?"

The woman shakes her head without speaking and returns to her reading.

"This is my first group, I was just wondering what it is like."

"Ah look, what's your name?"

"Shevonne."

"Look Shevonne, nothing against you but I would rather just sit here quietly and read."

"Okay, I understand but I figure you going to be talking in group right, saying all kinds of personal stuff. I thought maybe you wouldn't mind talking about the weather or some small talk before we jump into talking about how we hated our childhood or something. You know like warming up before a game."

The woman smiles reluctantly and says, "I suppose you have a point there uh Shevonne."

Shevonne whispers, "Are you someone famous, it looks like you're hiding."

"You don't have to be someone famous to hide Shevonne. We all do that in some way or another. Also you know part of the etiquette of these types of groups is anonymity. That's why we only use first names. People say a lot of private things and it is easier to say them to strangers."

"Oh, I see that yeah. But I can tell you are somebody special. You are so beautiful."

The woman says "So are you Shevonne but doesn't it bother you when that's all people see. It is like they can't get past it. It's like being rich, you never know if people like you for you or if it's because they want to share the wealth."

"Yeah it's like the real you inside isn't important, especially with men. The real you is like a distraction from the fantasy of you. Damn it's so hard being beautiful." Both woman laugh.

Shevonne says, "It's okay if I talk about me right?"

"Sure ok." The woman says "But probably nothing too heavy in the lobby."

"Girl it ain't nobody here but me and you and that woman hear everybody business all day, right?" The receptionist does not respond.

"Right now I got to choose between two men. I mean that's not why I'm here but that's what's on my mind."

"There are a lot of women that would like to have that problem Shevonne."

"Yeah but remember, we're beautiful. This happens to us all the time." They laugh again.

"So how is this different?" the woman asks.

Shevonne replies, "One guy is the love of my life. He has been there through the worst of the worse and he is smart, funny and brave."

"And the other guy?"

" Well you know he is the guy from tv, you know the Server, that's been on the news. I mean I had real demons in my head. I would not have been able to talk to you this way. I mean I have a lot of stuff in me and I know I'm not who I used to be yet. But the stuff that strangled me, that tortured my soul, is gone.

"I work for him now. I was at Riverside Church and at St. Patrick's with him Sunday. I just feel tingly and on the verge of something outstanding when I am in his presence. When I'm not, I feel less than normal and I don't feel safe."

"Sounds like quite a choice you have to make. I have seen the Server. In fact, I was in the crowd at St. Patrick's. I wasn't close to him when he spoke but his words resonate. They reverberate somewhere deep within me."

"Yes, yes. You must meet him." Shevonne says.

"I don't know. My guy is pretty jealous and protective."

"Oh I will tell your man Server is mine, you just coming to get some guidance." The woman smiles again.

"No need to do that but perhaps I will meet with him if you can arrange it." The woman says.

"I sure can. Write your name and e-mail on this."

Shevonne pulls a contact sheet from her bag. Other group members begin to enter. The receptionist says, "It's time."

They both get up. The woman gives her the contact sheet back. Shevonne looks at it and says "Thanks Tiffany."

As they approach the inner office where group therapy takes place, Tiffany remembers that all cell phones must be turned off. She notices that she has a call from Bloodworthy. She turns the phone off before entering the room, deciding to ignore the call. She really needs her therapy and thinks that maybe she has made a new friend.

Bloodworthy is not used to Tiffany ignoring his call. He wants to tell her about Anyman. He wants to share his excitement. He wants to undress her and see just how potent the new blood has made him. He hungers for the two girls and their blood. These girls are so beautiful and so near. But he wants the first time with them to be special. He wants Tiffany to arrange and participate in an orgy of blood and lust.

He does not think that Tiffany will object. He has seen other women, early in their relationship. He even brought them into their bedroom. He just does not want to see the deadness in Tiffany's eyes again. She has been even more amazing since the night of the storm when she pledged her soul to him. It will be all right he thinks. A man who aspires to immortality is not one to deny himself anything. So he will ask and she will adjust. He calls her again.

Tiffany and Shevonne have finished the group. They walk, talk, and decide to go to a nearby restaurant. They sit outside. Tiffany has become very interested in Shevonne's life. Shevonne is turning her head from side to side, looking around. She rarely came to Manhattan, maybe for a movie, shopping or to a club. Harlem is in Manhattan but feels like the Bronx. Downtown was different. This was not a place she would come to just to sit.

"You ok Shevonne?"

"Yeah, I usually don't hang out down here."

"Would you like to go somewhere different?" Tiffany asks

"No I'm good." She continues to look around.

Shevonne says, "You know I don't think I look at people when I'm down here shopping, I mean they might as well be buildings, just something you look at as part of the scenery, like checking out a movie. It's like now, I'm watching me in the movie but I know I won't be in it for long."

Tiffany smiles, "I like you Shevonne. Do you always say just what's on your mind?"

"For a while I didn't know what I was saying. I mean words would come out but it wasn't like I was saying it and I wouldn't know what I said. I would just look at whoever I was speaking with to know if it made sense or if I had stopped talking. I didn't know sometime."

"That must have been awful." Tiffany said.

Shevonne nods and looks around. She says to Tiffany, "I don't know if it is okay to talk about the things from group but it sounds like you still miss your mother a lot."

"Every day." Tiffany says. "She is still one of the most beautiful women I have ever seen. She was loving and kind. I have reviewed our life together in my mind. I did not know she was so unhappy."

"Shevonne says, "Most people think they can know you by what you show them. It's what you don't show that counts."

"Okay, Shevonne but don't you think that if you are around someone every day, you should know?"

"It sounds like you trying to blame yourself. You was just a little girl, you couldn't done nothing even if you knew." Tiffany gets tears in her eyes.

She puts her hands on top of Shevonne's and says "Thank you."

Tiffany's phone vibrates.

"Is that your man?" Shevonne asks.

"Yes."

"Sounds like he is blowing up your phone. Sounds like you need to give him his medicine."

Tiffany realizes Shevonne is talking about sex.

"Believe me its' extra strength and he doesn't miss a dose but I'm not a 24 hour pharmacy."

"I got to go anyway Tiffany; I got to get to Server. Next time you come hang out with me, I'll show you how we do things in the Bronx."

They give each other a hug and Tiffany pays for a cab for Shevonne. The cab driver balks at having to go to the Bronx but Tiffany gives him an extra ten.

"Yes Cleo." Tiffany says.

"I need to see you now." He says,

"I am on my way." She responds.

When Tiffany arrives, Cleo is in his robe. He walks over to her excited and hugs her. He tells her about Anyman, his excitement about the blood and asks if she notices anything different about him.

She gives him a thorough looking over and says,
"You do look like you lost ten pounds and your look more energetic."

His enthusiasm is reducing some of her annoyance at being summoned like a servant.

"Yes Cleo you look great. Can you get more blood?" She asks.

"I purchased two young virgins with special bloodlines. I am keeping them in a cabin upstate. They are accessible but removed from public scrutiny. I want you to be able to share their blood with me. It will keep you young and beautiful and full of energy."

"I will keep that in mind. What do they look like?"

"They look nubile and innocent."

"And you want to change that, I suppose?"

"Yes" Cleo says without hesitation, "I do. I want to see them in deerskin miniskirts and moccasins as if they are hunting wild beasts. I want to see them soaping up in the shower with rich lather, exciting each other before I open the door and surprise them with my knife. I want you to buy them sexy clothes, place them in exotic settings and teach them to please me."

Tiffany looks at him with sadness for an instant, then seconds later with anger and finally with cold resignation.

"Of course," She says. "Let me shower and change and I will get started on that."

Bloodworthy says, "Buy something new for yourself, something I haven't seen. I want our first time to be special." Tiffany does not answer. She goes in her room, sits in the dark, and wonders why no one loves her.

Shevonne returns to see Server. When she arrives he is involved a conversation with Terry Stiles.

"Server I am concerned that the number of threatening letters and e-mails are rising. I want to set up protection for you."

"What did you have in mind?" Server responds.

"I had experience in special forces with protecting important people who were potential targets. I have headed recon and I have done crowd surveillance. When I headed the Vets group, the government spied on us electronically and we came up with some protective measures."

"Terry I appreciate what you offer me and the love that is at the heart of your suggestion but I trust the father to protect me. If God decides it is my time to die, it does not matter what you or I do. If God wants me to live there is nothing our enemies can do to harm us. The people must learn to trust in God and have faith. They cannot think that I am afraid. They are spending $708 billion dollars a year on defense because they are frightened.

"They are spending their personal income to hide in gated communities because they live in fear of people who are different from them. Their money could be used to help the poor and the sick. They might insist upon it if they were not so afraid."

"Yes Server that is part of your mission as you have described it to us but what if my mission is to protect you. What if God's plan was for me to come to you and for you to use me."

Server thought about this for a moment. The bible is full of men who were role players in God's plan. Server replied, "There can be no violence in my name. I do not want or need your protection. You must accept that your help if discovered could make me ineffective, appear inauthentic and that would destroy me as certainly as an assassin's bullet. I want you to bear this in mind and meditate on God's plan for you."

Terry bows and withdraws. Shevonne has been waiting eagerly. When she sees Terry leave, she moves like a track star that has just heard the starter pistol.

"Server, I'm back. Can I help you with anything."

Server is still a little afraid of Shevonne. His immediate feeling was to tell her to go. But his words to Terry to trust and have faith in God still ring in his ears.

He asks her to have a seat and points to the chair behind his desk. They are working and talking together when they hear a disturbance. Several of the Servants led by Terry have confronted and detained Cleverness at the main door.

"Get the fuck off of me." He is yelling as Shevonne and Server rush out.

"Get back in the office." Terry instructs Server as he and Shevonne approach.

"Let him go." Server instructs as Cleverness continues to try to release his arms. When released, he takes a swing at Terry who ducks and then blocks the second punch.

Shevonne yells for Cleverness to stop and Terry steps back and says, "I apologize sir. I should not have grabbed you. I hope that you will forgive me."

Cleverness is already upset that Shevonne is wasting so much time with Server. Now this guy has pissed him off. He is sure though that the only way he will be able to stop Terry is to shoot him and he has too much money to make to get locked up over some bullshit.

"You tell me to come down here on Wednesday and I come and these motherfuckers grab me. Fuck it I came like I said I would. I'm out!"

"Wait" Server, says, "I deeply apologize. Lenny get your friend something to eat. Please come in and join us." Lenny smiles, nods, and reassures Cleverness.

Shevonne grabs his arm and kisses him on the cheek "Sorry baby, it won't happen again."

Cleverness goes in and they shut the door. He has calmed down. Server continues to reassure Marcus and reminds him of some of the humorous situations they have experienced together. Marcus smiles eventually and says, "Yeah I remember you and Shevonne crossing the street going to Burger King and trying to look all inconspicuous. Now that shit was funny!"

Shevonne says "Don't say shit..ooops." she extends her hand to Server's shoulder and apologizes. When she touches Server the smile leaves Marcus face.

"Don't tell me what to do Shevonne. When you were walking around doing all kinds of crazy shit I was there helping you. I was not criticizing your ass. Remember that?"

Server can see that Marcus is upset and knows why.

"Shevonne, why don't you let Marcus and I talk alone? Maybe afterwards you can show him around."

Shevonne starts to protest but thinks better of it, bows and leaves. When the door closes Marcus says, "Yo I appreciate what you did for my girl and all but now it's like you got her under some spell. I never get to see her anymore."

"She is just grateful, Marcus. Believe me I have no romantic interest in Shevonne."

"Yeah" Marcus said, "Then what was that weird stuff that happened to you after Shevonne rubbed against your dick on the couch?"

Server responded, "Let me ask you something. Why do you talk like that. Your cousin Racine is brilliant, and she says that you are one of the smartest people she has ever met. So why do you talk like that?"

"I don't know about all that but I am smart enough to know that you didn't answer my question. But ok I'll answer you first. If you worked in the science field, you would use their jargon or whatever. If you were speaking to an audience of dockworkers, you might not use a lot of polysyllabic words and you might not dress in a suit. You might have your sleeves rolled up. It ain't no different. Where I live I dress and use the lexicon and morphology of the street, Straight hood, nothing soft but smooth like butter, baby. Okay it's your turn. What's up?"

"My answer is I don't know. There was something about her on top of me that made me feel disordered. I felt like I had jumped off a mountain and I was two feet from the ground. Yet there was something worse than the impact, something worse that my body breaking into pieces that would be unleashed if I could not have thrown her off me."

"Wow you are truly, truly scared of pussy. Aren't you?"

Server smiles a weak smile and says, "So you see you have nothing to fear."

"Naw man, don't play a player. You must think you talking to a kid. You know you control a woman through her mind. Even if she never had a good fuck and you give her Rembrandt dick, she will leave you for a man that stimulates her imagination."

"Yes Marcus but I fear the passion that Shevonne desires and I love the person I am now. It makes no sense that I would risk my greatest love for my greatest fear." Marcus is now reassured.

"So what do you want from me. Why did you ask me to come here today?"

"I have a strong intuition that you hold the answer to the one I seek. I have felt that since the first time I met you at the police station."

Marcus nods, "Okay but why today?"

"I just feel these things Marcus and I trust that they are coming from God."

"So the guy you are looking for, what does this guy look like?" Marcus asks.

"I have never seen him?" Server says.

"Well what you know about him?"

Server replies, "I know he is evil, I know that he is so evil that I will sense his presence if he is within one hundred yards of me. He is been sent by the father of lies; his very essence is deception and he leads men to sully their souls. I will smell the carnage, I will see the blood."

"Okay you got to speak-a-de-English. I don't know what the fuck you are talking about and all that shit you talking don't give me a clue how to help you."

"Are you supposed to see anyone today?" Server asks.

"Yeah but that doesn't concern you." Marcus says.

"You are a man of your word. Remember our deal."

Marcus nods. "I know but I'm not going to let you fuck up my money. I got real business I got to handle. It would be too hard to explain you."

"Then let's talk about it on the way to the studio."

"What do you mean?" Marcus asks.

"I am going to be on your cousin's news show today."

"Yeah, yeah she told me about that. Yeah alright I'll go down there and surprise her."

"Thank you Marcus. Oh and Marcus just like you need to communicate a certain way to your associates, mine expect for you to talk to me respectfully, can you do that for me?"

"Fuck yeah. Naw I'm just kidding. I won't disrespect you in front of your peeps. Just don't expect that shit in private." Server shakes his head and smiles.

Chapter 12

Cleo Bloodworthy has been blindfolded for the last ten miles. He is jarred by bump after bump on this very rocky road. They are driving uphill. The air gets cooler as they rise and their vehicle seems to struggle more to keep its' upward momentum.

Tiffany and Cleo had some difficult moments in the weeks following her introduction to the two girls. She seemed withdrawn and pensive. This made Cleo ruder and more demanding. He required her to do demeaning acts, in and out of bed. He enjoyed his power over her at first, choosing to crush her defiance. But she was no common woman and he no common man.

At his request, he could have ten submissive women at his disposal. He could kill them all and start over again. She could move on to the next rich man and any of them would be grateful to have her. She had a way of making her value known.

He wanted Tiffany's mind as well as her body. He longed to have her completely but he was not willing to give up the girls. So he started lavishing Tiffany with gifts, he spent more time with her and gave her more independence. She appeared to be genuinely more receptive to his advances and asked him to clear his weekend schedule for a surprise trip. The road has become even bumpier and the jeep became more difficult to maneuver. Momentarily, he became concerned that she was still angry and intends to harm him leaving his body abandoned in the mountains somewhere. As he was thinking about removing the blindfold, the vehicle pulls to a stop.

"Get up." Tiffany said.

He raises his arm to remove the blindfold but she says "No."

She grabs his arm to and pulls him from the vehicle. She moves away from him and then says in a loud voice, "Ok take it off now, you bastard."

When Bloodworthy removes the blindfold, Tiffany is pointing a pistol at him and two big men, Samoan he thinks, are flanking her. Behind them is a huge cave. It is deep and foreboding. Darkness is descending and the sun has disappeared behind the clouds. He unconsciously surveys all that is around him. He wonders if this is his last look at the world.

"Let's go." She says.

They enter the cave. The two Samoans are behind her and she walks with the gun pointed at his back. She taunts him as they move further into the cave.

The Samoans are silent, Cleo is too tense to try anything, and thinks begging would be futile. There is still light from the outside of the cave but it gets darker as they go further inside. Tiffany stumbles and the gun flies toward Bloodworthy. He picks it up as the Samoans draw their guns.

They start to fire toward him and he fires back and retreats further into the cave. He runs as fast as he can until he sees a light. The cave has widened and it appears he must go further down and to the right. If he goes straight or to the left, there is only total darkness. The floor of the cave is very uneven and he has heard animals moving in the dark. Yes, he will walk towards the flame he sees in the distance.

As he gets closer, he can see a wood fire on a ledge. He moves even closer and sees a boy, thin and about ten years old. The boy is beckoning him, waving vigorously for him to come.

He looks around for some sign of danger and seeing none, he approaches the boy. Before he can ask him anything the boy disappears. Cleo is in a stone corridor lit by torches on the wall.

He is terrified of what lies ahead but knows that there is certain danger if he confronts the Samoans. He moves forward unsteadily, his knees shake nervously, as does his hand as he points the gun in front of him. He hears voices. He places the second hand on the gun to steady it.

There is an opening in the wall of the cave. It is about sixteen feet and wide. It is completely dark and the voices stop as he makes his approach.

He yells, "I have a gun. Come out now or I will start shooting."

Nothing. He grabs a nearby torch from the wall. Imagines flicker in and out of darkness from the corner of the room.

"You saved us", they say. "Now we must do anything you ask."

He can see the two girls in animal skins, their breasts barely covered. They move toward him and start kissing him and removing his clothes.

He smiles and yells in relief and delight "Tiffany."

She moves out of the shadows holding a wine glass and smiling. She shoots the blank gun up in the air as the Samoans enter the room carrying a bed with roses and gourmet chocolates. Now stripped completely naked, he says, "There is no one like you."

Tiffany pushes him back onto the bed and pours the blood-wine on his belly. The girls lick frantically. She caresses him and tickles his testicles.

"I know." She says. "I know."

As Bloodworthy enjoys his fantasy, Noble is living his dream. He is back on top. When he airs, his ratings are the highest they have ever been. The producers are talking about new opportunities for him and his star, Server. Racine has her own show because of her talent and Noble's new power. Noble also promised her a segment with Server for her show's premiere. This will guarantee high ratings.

Racine was now insisting that Noble work with the journalist at Le Plume to remake media. He had hoped that developing her new show would keep her so busy she would not have time to bother him. Racine's news show is 'Just the Facts, Ma'am.' She envisioned a value –based show that blended information with emotion. She wanted to move hearts and restore minds. She would be provocative in her presentation and flawless in her fact checking. If Noble was not ready for change, she would lead by example. She had decided to use Server in her opening show as planned. She is wary of his unknown past and her journalistic training makes her cautious. She knows that if Server has any minor fault in his past, it would be the story of the day, every day for weeks. He would become the Bernie Madoff of religion.

She also knows that whatever and whoever Server is, he is sincere. He resonates with unselfish love. She trusts her instincts and the life lessons she learned from her parents growing up in Racine, Wisconsin.

Racine's ancestors were escaped slaves who fled to the town of Racine, Wisconsin through the Underground Railroad. The town was strongly Abolitionist. So much so, that when a slave Joshua Glover, was arrested in Milwaukee, one hundred men from Racine stormed the jail to free him. One of the hundred men was her ancestor, Turner Parks. After Glover was set free, Turner cried for hours.

He had experienced much pain and brutality at the hands of his owner. Everyone he knew had lived an empty life filled with misery and despair. His family had escaped to Racine but he never felt safe. In his dreams, he heard the dogs barking. During the day, he walked in the shadows. With the freeing of Glover he finally felt something long forgotten, he felt hope.

He told his wife that the last time he had hoped was years before Glover when they were still on the plantation. It was the first time he saw snow. It was like the clouds were coming down piece by piece. Maybe Jesus was coming he thought. Instead, snow just made the ground colder and made his bones ache as he did his work. No hope was not like snow. Hope made him feel warm inside. The snow melted in a few days, hope stayed in his heart. Hope was in his eyes as he told the story of the freeing of Joshua Glover to his children.

Since then, one person in each generation has been named Racine, named after the place that gave Turner Parks hope. It is what hope means to Racine when she hears it. She cannot bear false witness to it.

Her mother and father were strongly middle-class. They could have afforded to move from Racine long ago. They earned far more than their neighbors did but they elected to stay. They were loyal, to their city, their family and their ideals. Many of her Dad's siblings had moved away, following big paychecks, more culture or opportunity. Marcus parents moved when he was an infant. They always returned with great fanfare and brought the best gifts. Marcus father always drove the cars he called "Imported excellence."

Unfortunately, they had little time for Marcus. His family lived in a great home in Westchester. He had the great grades. He won the regional science fair once and was accepted to Horace Mann in Riverdale. But he was always adventurous. When Racine visited, Marcus always took her to the South Bronx. As kids, they were always exploring abandoned buildings and factories. She remembered curved light through broken windows, piercing the darkness. They saw huge rats poking their heads out of grey crevices and then waddling along the edge of the wall.

They went further and further into shadows, not knowing what lurked beyond the next turn. They both loved this type of excitement, dangerous and unexplored. It is why he liked the street life and why she became an investigative reporter.

"Good evening friends and neighbors, I am honored to sit before you here today and bring you the news. It is the culmination of my life's dream and a responsibility I take very seriously.

"Because I take my duty to you so seriously, I will tell you if corporations are taking risks that endanger your home and your job. I will let you know if your government is planning to go to war under false pretenses. I will give you information on votes that can affect your life in enough time for you to do something about it.

"I will not bring you horse race politics. I will not act as though there are two sides to all things. Some things are good ideas and others are bad. I will find the facts and I will check the facts. I will be your advocate and I will be your friend.

"I remember Oprah had just lost the top ratings spot to Jerry Springer. She was number one for years. Instead of going more sensationalistic and trying to compete with the banality of his show, she refused. She chose spiritual and health topics and created a book club. She trusted the people.

"60 minutes for years was the number one watched show in America. People chose quality when given a choice. Now I realize it is a different time. I have a colleague who regularly chants "Ratings baby, ratings." Corporate owned media crave advertisers and cable news stations want to win time slots more than they want to inform viewers. We must keep cost down. How better to do that than to eliminate foreign correspondents, investigative reporting and research departments?

"It is far cheaper to have 'experts' appear each day. So you can have one expert tell you the earth is flat and the other tell you it is round. We are asked to hear what the left thinks and what the right thinks. Then the newsman will thank them and conclude that each side has a valid point. I sit there and hope he falls off the earth.

"So I welcome you to join me for news like the old days presented in a new time. Providing the information that will keep you and your family safe and informed is my sacred trust."

Racine does an excellent job interviewing her guest and reporting the news. Server is the last interview and they walk out together. They are discussing the show when Marcus sneaks up behind her and grabs her.

She is startled and turns her head. When she sees it is him, she jostles free and smacks him on the shoulder.

"You know you almost got hurt right?"

"Yeah I know you're tough."

"Don't let the clothes fool you. I can scrap like the old days."

"Yeah" Marcus says sarcastically, "That's the word on the street."

They both laugh. Marcus says, "Cous, all jokes aside, you were like magic out there. I mean even with this freak of nature here you held your own."

He looks at Server and says "No offense." And hugs her again.

Racine was happy a moment ago but she is sparkling now. Being with Marcus made this experience bigger and more luminescent. He was witness to her dream in its infancy. He knew her when she had held the hair brush in her hand pretending it was a microphone. Hell, she had interviewed him that way.

It will be great to talk to her colleagues, she thinks, celebrate at dinner, they understand the business. It will be an honor to go to Le Plume and have legends give her praise. It will be the grand delight of life in the moment. But in Marcus hug, in his words, the little girl is recognized, acknowledged and fulfilled.

"I wish I could stay and celebrate with you, Rae but I got to go." She gives him another hug.

"Thanks you being here meant a lot to me." As he leaves, Server also says goodbye.

"Where are you going?" She asks Server.

"Me and Marcus have business." He says. She looks at him quizzically.

"You and Marcus are hanging out together. Now that's a story!"

Chapter 13

Cleo is feeling better than he has in years. He has just returned from unexpected pleasure in the cave and his body is alive with new blood. He is deciding how to use his new energy when he gets good news from Congressman Anthony Moural.

"Hi Cleo, I have outstanding information for you." Genuflect will receive patents for all of the human genes it applied for. That means if anyone wants to test for the potential for mental illness, diabetes, alcoholism, arthritis or cancer they must pay Genuflect."

This is the news Bloodworthy had been waiting for. It was years in the making. He first began by genetically altering rice seeds and then eliminating all competing seeds. Farmers had to use his altered rice seed or nothing at all. He owned the patent. He had a virtual monopoly on rice in America.

Some had argued that seeds were living things and that no one should have a monopoly on seeds but he and his army of lawyers persevered. Farmers that resisted were arrested and Bloodworthy's considerable resources were used to kill their farms.

But this was better. Many years ago, Genuflect like other biotech companies were racing to map the human genome. As they "discovered" genes that could indicate diabetes, or types of cancer or any potential medical condition, they patented the discovery. So now, any doctor who wanted to test a patient to see if she had the gene that would potentially cause the disease had to pay Genuflect and pay thousands. Bloodworthy knew that owning the right to particular genes in the human body would be difficult. Fortunately, the Supreme Court decided that corporations could provide unlimited funding to political candidates and so he bought Congressman like A.Moural and a few Senators. Then he brought out the ORCS (Obnoxious Rubes Conserving Stupidity). This is what the opposition called the various organizations that Reversal' funded to march in the street and protest against socialism. They marched and the Pavlovian media reported for weeks that efforts to stop ownership of human genes were a government takeover of business rights and an attempt to make the country more socialist.

Moural was now reporting on the fruits of Cleo's labor as if it was he that had done the work. But since Cleo was in a great mood so he said.

"Good work Anthony. Glad to hear it. I look forward to celebrating soon with you and your wife." The Congressman was pleased that he was again in Bloodworthy's good graces.

"Certainly, certainly I look forward to it." They ended the call.

Cleo threw his hands in the air with glee. He thought about the billions to be made. His wealth was now immense. He was now a giant. No need to fly he thought, he now towered over men. God may have created man but he would own the patent. He felt in his bones that he had reached the summit of his existence as an ordinary man.

He knew these new patents would provide immeasurable wealth and power. Yet he would eventually become a frail, toothless and wrinkled thing watching all that he created blossom while he withered away. He vowed to dominate the human gene market and to find immortality in one year. He wanted these achievements while at the height of his power. One year he told himself. This must be done. But first there were some loose ends to clean up.

Bloodworthy had a hostage in his cabin in the woods. Brady and a few other mercenaries were guarding him but they would soon have to leave. Brady had a relative, a reporter, who was being held for ransom by Somali pirates. It was Brady's cousin. If he were not a close relative, Brady would not have disappointed Bloodworthy.

Cleo was forced to find someone, local, discreet and smart to guard the hostage and he knew just the man. He was a former employee and he used him for small criminal situations with good results. He would arrive just as Brady was leaving. Cleo was paying big money for this job but the hostage was priceless. Perhaps he would have thought his confidence in this man was misplaced if he knew what he was doing and who he was with.

"Okay you got me for a few hours." Marcus said, "What is it you want to do? You want to be a gangster. All that swami shit was just an act huh? You want to be a thug." Server smiles, Marcus continues.

"It's ok I really ain't got nothing heavy today. I got to pack some clothes, other than that we can hang out. Chills and thrills baby, that is how I roll, a day in the crazy life of Cleverness. You will..."

His phone rings and he holds up a finger to quiet Server as though he were the one talking. Marcus responds to his cell phone. It is one of Bloodworthy's men; the big, heavy man that came to Shevonne's apartment in the Bronx.

"Cleverness the man needs to move up the date. You need to get out there today."

"What you mean, I got plans today J.B."

"The soldier had to leave early, sumpin about the situation changin. He's waiting there. The man said send somebody to get your shit later but you got to get out there now."

"Alright, okay I'm on my way."

Marcus ends the call and looks at Server and says, "Look some really important stuff has come up. I got to drop you off."

"No Marcus. I will go with you." Server replies,

"Look freak, I mean look, I can't fuck this up. Not only is this guy dangerous, he has an endless pot of gold. I am not going to risk pissing this guy off. We can do this another day." Cleverness begins making a U-turn.

"You gave your word. I thought that meant something."

Cleverness pulls over and starts banging his fist on the steering wheel. He has done many things in his life, he has lied and conned people but he has never uttered the phrase "I promise", and not followed through.

Marcus father was always busy. He would promise vacations that never happened; movies and ballgames got canceled at the last minute. He remembered always being the last to be picked up from school. He especially remembered when his father was supposed to pick him up after an away game. The coach and his friends on the team told him to ride with them. He refused. His dad promised he would pick him up and that they would hang out together at Sliding Home, a sports bar a few miles away.

He was 16 and his dad had always treated him like a kid. He knew his father would not let him drink alcohol but this was a coming of age event. Sliding Home was a hangout for his dad's cool friends. These were the guys from the life he never let the family see. Marcus knew that even his mother had never been there.

The game had gone great. He scored thirty points and grabbed ten rebounds. He had hurried to get dressed after the game. He was the first one out of the locker room.

As the last car pulled away and he was left standing at the curb, he waved goodbye and resisted any thought that his father would let him down again. Marcus had made his father reconfirm his promise the night before and again in the morning.

"Are you sure dad?"

"Yes son I promise."

As Marcus stood on the corner waiting, ten guys rounded the corner. Two of them were from the team they had just defeated, their archrival. He had time to run, if he ran now. Every impulse told him to do just that. He stood still though because he could see a car about two blocks away coming toward them. It was green like his dad's car but it was hard to see it. The sun had gone down and it was just getting dark. He stayed.

Once the guys saw who he was they ran at him. The first boy shoved him and then they pinned his back against the roll-gate of an abandoned store and began punching him. The last thing he saw before losing consciousness was the smiling family in the car as it passed by. He was not sure if the car had been green at all.

"Look man", Marcus said to Server. "I'm keeping my word. I'm just telling you- look you supposed to be all loving and compassionate and shit. Just let me out the deal. When I get back, I'll give you a week if you want. I'll even be one of your Servers for a while. I just gotta do this alone."

Server looked at Marcus and placed his hand on his shoulder.

"Marcus in the spiritual world these things are not random. When I chose today, I did not know why. I still do not know why I chose today. God wanted me to be with you today the same way he wanted me to be at that bank robbery, or at the police station when I met you. I have no choice in this. I am going where you go."

Marcus was furious. He drove toward his destination like a maniac at first. Then realizing that he could not afford to be arrested, he slowed down and on the long ride he eventually lost some of his rage.

"Look" he said to Server "I am going to let you out about a mile away. They can't see me pull up with anybody. It could blow the whole deal. Do you have a cell phone?" Server shakes his head.

"Here take mine. I will call you once they are gone." Server is concerned that this is a trick and that he will be left stranded. Marcus sees the concern and says, "This is legit man. I give you my word...Damn I go to stop saying that."

Server exits. Marcus drives to the large isolated cabin. Server sits and meditates until he receives the call. He walks to the cabin and looks around as he approaches. The cabin is large but not so large that it causes unwanted attention. The windows reflect the sunlight so Server cannot see inside until he is close to the house. There are cameras on the roof, which rotate and follow his movement. He reaches the door and is about to knock when Marcus opens the door and lets him in.

He tells Server, "Take a look around, get something to eat if you want. Come downstairs when you finish." He points at a door. "Over there." Marcus heads for the door and Server can hear him walking down steps.

Server likes the like high beamed ceilings and the generous sunlight from the huge back window. Beyond the back of the house is about two acres of trees and then a cliff, a long steep drop and then a narrow creek where water ably navigates small rocks and debris.

The kitchen is large and modern with a fully stocked fridge. Server makes a plate of salmon and salad and heads for the steps. The steps are large and the hall is dark. There are two flights of steps. The second set of stairs is longer and leads to a large open room. There are a four sofas, of different colors and eras, a large flat screen tv, and several chairs. In one of the chairs is a tall, thin man. His legs are shackled like the old chain gangs and his hands are taped behind his back with gray masking tape.

Marcus is eating a bowl of chips, mixed with pretzels and watching television.

"Sit down man, make yourself at home." He says as if oblivious to the bound man a few feet from him.

Server pulls up a chair and with his plate on his lap and scoots over and whispers, "Who is that?"

Marcus looks at Server and says in a normal voice. "Get yourself a tray man you don't have to sit your food on your lap and move over. Why are you sitting so close to me with all this room?"

Server again asks quietly "Who is that?"

Marcus looks away from the television for a moment and says, "Look this is want you wanted. If you stay here, you are taking part in kidnapping just like me. You can leave now, hell you should leave now. You could get life in prison for this and you ain't even getting paid."

Server said, "Let me know who he is and what is going on and I will decide. Maybe I am supposed to free him."

Marcus responds, "Maybe I am supposed to bust a cap in your ass. Listen you ain't freeing nobody."

Server pulls up a chair near Anyman. Anyman opens his eyes. He has been in a deep, trance –like state. His eyes slowly focus. He slowly reacquaints himself with his grim surroundings. He sees Marcus, the flat screen, the old and dirty furniture and then he senses the presence beside him and exclaims, "Oh no they have got you too. All is lost, all is lost."

Server responds, "What do you mean? Who are you?"

"I am the beginning of the bloodline of man. My blood is in every man. When the Holy Spirit first entered man, it mingled with the blood I possess."

Marcus gets up and checks the tape and chains that hold Anyman. "I am going to move your chair so that I can watch you and the game."

He leans Anyman's chair and drags it between the flat screen and his chair. He motions for Server to come to him. This time he whispers. "I gave you my word that's why you're here. Now I want you to promise me that you won't try to release this guy if I let you two talk."

Server thinks for a moment and then responds. "I will say this; I will not use deceit or trickery. If I find he must be released. It is you who will do it."

Marcus chuckles "Okay that works for me since there is no way in hell I will let him go."

Server says, "I will also let you know if he is trying to escape but I want you to let us talk privately." Marcus thinks this is a good deal. Server will watch him and he does not care what they are talking about.

"Yeah alright but keep it down." Server moves Anyman even further back in the room. They are in the corner and it is darkly lit.

Server sits and says, "Tell me more." Anyman responds.

"There are a small number of us who have a direct bloodline to our beginnings. Over millenniums, despots, kings, thugs and saints have sought us out, thinking our blood to be valuable."

"Is it?" Server asks

"It has been for those who know its value. Some sought us out thinking us to be demons. They sought to burn us. Others thought to sacrifice us to please their Gods. We have had our blood sprinkled on crops, tossed in the eyes of blind men and buried with the dead so that they may be reborn in the afterlife. But weather saint or sinner, for good or evil most sought to kill or imprison us."

"So which is intended this time?" Server asks.

"The man he works for seeks to hold me because he thinks my blood is the purest. He intends to use my blood until he can find the blood of an angel, a living prophet or is bitten three times by a Vampire." Server thinks immediately about his mission and the cave of the Vampire.

"Do you know where Vampires exist?" The question surprises Anyman, it is not the response he expected.

"Why do you want to know this of all things?"

"It is my mission to do the will of God. He has directed me to go the cave of the Vampire and stop the bleeding."

"I know where Vampires exist. They live in small isolated communities as do those I lead. Some live among you and others are just part Vampire like the one who holds us captive."

"The one who imprisons you is part Vampire?"

"Yes, he lusts for the life of the immortal and is using my blood and the blood of two virgins to deter aging until he can conquer death. I thought that is why he had brought you here."

"What do you mean?"

"You are a prophet. You are what he needs to fulfill his destiny."

"How do you know that I am He." Anyman looks at him quizzically.

"You are not He. It is He who sends all, it is He that sent you. You are here to restore balance. Dark energy overwhelms our planet and the universe. It is by nature weak but is multiplying and overtaking the light. The light needs virtue, charity, faith and truth for its existence. All are fading from our hearts and minds. Ten thoughts of empathy overwhelm ten thousand evil thoughts. Yet even at this rate evil is winning. It has been said, 'People do not want to do good. They want to feel good about what they do.' People misled by evil imagine that the hate and intolerance they feel is God's will. They have no need to be virtuous. Virtue requires discipline, sacrifice, dedication and spiritual growth. Instead, they submit to their worst passions and their religious and political leaders tell them they are doing good. So they feel moral in doing evil, even superior. This has been the greatest ruse of the King of Lies."

"Thank you." Server says.

"For what?"Anyman answers.

"Not long ago I was a bum, a homeless man. I ate with rats and sat with men who were tortured by voices in the heads. I mean I always knew the voices I heard were real and that I was supposed to work for God but until now, I had doubt. I did not know if I was chosen or insane."

"Rest assured the things that trouble you matter to men, not God. It is important that humankind realize that status and riches are not the way to truth. The most they can bring is temporary happiness and a craving for more. They never bring peace. The peace of the cross is letting go. The spiritual power of the cross lets you rest in joy. It means death of the whims of the body, its fears and its frailty. The peace of the cross means the resurrection of the vital and eternal association with the creator. It lasts through life and after death. It is why Jesus taught us to love the poor. What can be gained but virtue, the poor have no things. No my friend, you are sane and right where you were meant to be."

Server's eyes swelled with tears, a mixture of joy and relief. "How do you know such things?"

"My people have a rich oral tradition. Our wisdom spans the globe has accumulated for millenniums. We have taken the best of humanity and examined and preserved it. We are keenly aware of the rhythms of the earth, the nature of man and the power of the supernatural"

"Will you help to find the one I seek?" Anyman replies, "First I must ask you a question. You do not seem to be a prisoner. How is it that you are here?"

"I was drawn to your captor," He points at Marcus. "I felt that he would lead me to the vampire. I now think he was supposed to lead me to you. You are the reason God sent me here. "

"Perhaps. I was relieved to discover that you were not a prisoner. I hope you are here to release me."

Marcus had been listening. "I hear you both. No one is going anywhere. Server do I still have your word?"

"Yes" Server says.

Marcus continues "And this dude anyman, anywhere, anyclues whatever. He aint all that holy. He sold two girls into slavery for cash.

So to me, he's a pimp. If he got all the wisdom since time began and shit, why he pimpin virgins to rich dudes for cash?"

Anyman asks Server, "Have you agreed to keep me prisoner?"

Server says, "Is what he said about the girls true?"

Marcus chuckles to himself. He thinks what if Server is a prophet and Anyman is an ancient Wiseman. He has just manipulated them both the same way you got too teens to fight each other on the block.

Then he truly wonders what if they really are who they say they are. He has minimized it but he has certainly seen Server do some phenomenal things. He knows that the boss paid a lot for Anyman's virgins and the boss ain't no fool. Maybe he is the real deal. Could he really kill either one of them if he had to kill them? He didn't know. One thing was for certain though, they had to think so.

There is a pounding at the door. They all turn their heads. Marcus races up the steps followed by Server. Three swarthy looking men with machine guns confront them. Outside of the large back window, they see a helicopter near the cliff, its rotors' racing.

"Where is our leader?" The large man asks aiming the gun at Marcus eyes. Marcus knows these are not men to play with. He says,

"He is downstairs."

They keep their guns on Marcus as he leads them downstairs.

"Release him." One of the men demands. Marcus cuts the tape and uses the key to remove the shackles from Anyman's ankles. They make Marcus drop the knife that he has used to cut the tape. One of the armed men takes them upstairs as others talk to Anyman. Server and Marcus stand silently awaiting their fate.

Anyman quickly moves to the top of the steps and emerges rubbing his wrists. He looks at them both and says only "Bring them." Anyman's bodyguards motion with their rifles for Server and Marcus to follow them and they head for the chopper. The helicopter lifts off swirling debris into the open door of the cabin. As it leaves, a limousine pulls up to the front of the house. Bloodworthy watches the chopper fade into the distance, shaking his fist and cursing its departure.

Chapter 14

"Please let him up." Server pleads.

Anyman asks, "Why did you agree to keep me captive?"

"I did agree to keep you captive. Although I did not even know that you were there until I arrived. I knew that I was destined to be here today and Marcus would only let me stay on the condition that I agree not to free you. I told him that when the time was right, he would set you free but I always intended to see you unbound and unharmed."

"Let me go!" Marcus screams as he dangles upside down from a rope attached to the chopper. The guards sit motionless.

The pilot is laughing and yells, "I don't think you want them to let you go." They all ignore the pilot and Marcus.

Anyman looks deeply into Server's eyes and says, "I understand and I believe you."

Server hears more of Marcus terrified screams, muffled and distorted by the wind.

"Can we please let him up." Server pleads.

"In due time." Anyman replies.

"What will you do with him?" Server asks.

"He needs understanding, we will provide it. I think we both sense that he is a strong spirit that could not see beyond his surroundings. We will guide him towards a better destiny."

"I am glad you have decided to see his value and not his pain. Thank you." Server says.

"Are you not concerned what we will do with you?" Anyman asks.

"You know me as a prophet. I know you will return me to my destiny."

"Yes, yes but first I will show you what I would not show the man you seek. I will show you Vampires."

"If he is the one I seek, why not bring me to him. Why do I need to see Vampires?"

Anyman replies, "Vampires are gaining prominence. They are getting stronger as humanity declines. They are targeting those of virtue because virtuous blood is potent. One drop can satisfy their lust for months. They seek them out like the club who dine on the meat of endangered species. Vampires also target them because they want evil and ignorance to flourish. I want you to be able to spot them, to smell them, to sense them."

"Are we going there now?"

"We will spend a week with my people. I have leadership duties; I will attend to them and then recuperate. This trip has been more taxing than I had anticipated. I will get your friend on the right path and then I will introduce you to my family. I don't think they have ever met a prophet."

"And then?"

"And then we will go on a discreet journey to meet these beings that suck the essence out of us, distort our thinking and deaden our compassion. We will observe them from a distance and I will introduce you to one of them, a traitor to their cause. He will prepare you for your battle with the man called Bloodworthy."

Server says "But I thought you said he was not a Vampire."

"He is not but he is from a direct line of blood. Usually a man or woman must be bitten three times to become a vampire. He needs to be bitten only once by a vampire or have your blood and he can be as destructive as Hitler. As he is now, he is indirectly responsible for thousands of deaths and distorting the minds of millions. For the good of man, he must be stopped."

Server nods and then says, "Can we…" and before he can finish Anyman says to the guard, "Pull up the rope and let him in."

The guards pull the rope up and Marcus scurries into the helicopter moving as far away from the door as the guards will allow. Marcus is still terrified and is shaking. The guards move toward him to tie his hands. Initially he resists but they threaten to put him outside again, so he cooperates. The pilot tells Anyman that they are fifteen minutes from their destination. He nods. They land at a rural airport where a private plane awaits them.

They duck down to avoid the helicopter blades and move quickly to the plane. The plane is bigger than it appears on the outside and it is so clean it is bright. The crew moves immediately to Anyman, including a doctor who asks to examine him as soon as he will allow. Anyman waves him off. He proceeds to a circular area where he invites Server to sit. Once they are in the air, he commands the guards to untie Marcus. Marcus realizes his situation and does not attempt to escape. There is nowhere to go. Anyman invites him to sit with him and Server.

"Where are we going?" Marcus asks.

"Sit down, young man. You are about to begin a journey to self-awareness that will change your life and elevate your being. We might as well begin now."

Marcus sits but is wary. Anyman continues,

"These are the seeds of wisdom from which your mind and soul will blossom. There are seven. I will tell you now of five. You cannot comprehend the other two until you have been many years on the path.

"First, there is a great ocean of truth. I will teach you to see truth in all its forms as clearly as you see water. In many lands, people are dying of spiritual thirst. Having been deceived, they drink water filled with impurities. It is killing their bodies and drying their souls.

"Second, we will teach you to be truly brave. Much of our anger and hatred begins with fear. In America, it is the immigrants who will take our jobs, the terrorists will kill us; the gays will make us gay. We also fear any attack of the ego, any criticism we face must be met by defense or an even harsher attack. You were born in the land of the free and the home of the brave yet your individual and collective cowardice imprisons your mind and depletes your freedom.

"Third, you are all full with pride. You must lack self-importance. If we spent more time thinking about the needs of others or our love of God, we would enjoy benefits beyond belief instead of an empty, self-absorbed existence. The ever escalating need for pleasure combined with mind-numbing work to support it, can never be satisfying.

"If then in desperation one turns to religion and selects the wrong church, one finds that you have allowed it to be distorted and polluted because of fear, there is nothing holy there, nothing to sustain you. So you become resigned, living in apathy, seeking distraction until death.

"Fourth, you must accept the oneness of all things. The devil seeks to divide and conquer. We are all creatures of all mighty God. All of us have the potential for good and evil whether Black, White, Northern or Southern, Baptist or Buddhist. It seems childishly simple but appearance, religion or country of origin does not make us bad. It is the evil thoughts and feelings that we allow to seep into minds and hearts that determine who we are. The rest is simply lies that benefit the national, corporate and pseudo-religious leaders that exploit them. Our souls come from and return to God. The soul is invisible and free of the things we give meaning. Yet, attached to the soul like barnacles and visible to God are the ideas and emotions, which encumber it. Anger, intolerance and greed weigh down the soul, forcing its descent and attracting it to the father of lies.

"Fifth, we are spiritual beings using a body to enhance experience. We are not bodies with souls; we are souls wearing bodies. Therefore, we must live more spiritually. We have made our bodies stronger and safer. We have done amazing things to increase our brainpower. Yet spiritually, we are babies. We must pray and meditate more. We must also realize that we vibrate, that we are a force like gravity. We are magnetic and electric. We must build our capacity to dispel negative energy in the universe and to create and manipulate force. If we do, we will end hunger and disease and move closer to the creator."

Marcus is very impressed by what he hears and surprised at the love he feels emanating from Server and the man who had just ordered the scariest moments of his life. He heads to the back of the plane and sits quietly weeping.

Server and Anyman sit for many hours talking, meditating and planning. By the time they arrive at Anyman's homeland, they have synchronized their minds and they have jointly envisioned Bloodworthy's defeat.

When they land a caravan of cars greet them and they begin a two-hour journey. They come immediately to a tiny town that is only six blocks. It is barely modern and the roads are newly paved. They travel past the town toward miles and miles of small farms and a few shacks that advertise groceries or beer. After an hour, one can see only jungle and narrow dirt roads known to the driver and few others.

The road begins to curve and Server realizes that they are headed up a mountain on a winding, bumpy road. As they begin to reach the summit of the mountain, Server begins to see people busy in their tasks of ranching, building and working. They drive above these people and into more jungle. Marcus has been riveted to his seat, not knowing what to expect. He feels a little unsettled but he also feels that what he is seeing is somehow familiar.

The caravan heads towards the opening of a waterfall that has an opening as large as a ten story building and as wide as a football field. All the cars stop and put their vehicles in neutral. There is a loud whirring sound and then a click. The cars move forward as if on a conveyor belt. The mechanical whirring sound is overwhelmed by the thunderous sound of water pounding on the metallic extension that protects the vehicles as they roll slowly through the waterfall. It appears the vehicles will hit the stone surface behind the water when the stone surface opens allowing the cars to enter. A few dozen guards meet the cars. When it is clear that all is well, the guards permit the cars to pass.

As they proceed, Server and Marcus experience awesome simplicity. They smell the fragrance of flowers. The colors seem more vivid. It is as if they had dirty glasses on all their lives and they were suddenly cleaned. People are taller, thinner and happier.

Anyman lives in a modern castle. The exterior is the heavy, gray brick reminiscent of medieval Europe. The interior has ancient rugs from Persia, paintings from the Renaissance, ancient text encased in gold from Mali and Greek statues. There are eclectic, original works of art from every era and region of the earth.

Server and Marcus are housed in separate quarters reserved for important guests. Both men are tired and fall asleep almost immediately. The next day Marcus begins his training called Resurrection. He is first summoned to the Great Room where Anyman addresses him.

"Good Morning Marcus. Did you sleep well?"

"Yeah, I had some dreams but yeah I slept good."

"What did you dream about?" Anyman inquires.

"I was deep in the jungle using my hands to clear a path and trying to keep my feet from getting tangled in the vines. I did not want to trip but I did and when I fell I landed in the Bronx. When I stood up I was me but not me, you know how dreams are." Anyman nodded.

"Well I got up and I felt something on my ankles and I thought I still had vines on me but it was chains with a big metal ball like you see in cartoons or them old chain gang movies. I picked up the ball and I could see my face in it. Not like a reflection but like I was inside the ball and I was in pain. Then the face in the ball started to get all distorted like that painting The Scream. The ball became bigger and lighter and like a giant balloon. It picked me up and flew me around the South Bronx. I could see me at different ages and hear the voices of other people who were not there at the time those things were happening.

"Suddenly, the balloon burst and I fell through the sky into the perfect softness of my mother's lap. I heard her voice, that gentle comforting sound that memory had failed to produce for so many years."

Anyman asks, "What did she say?"

"See for yourself." Then she just rocked me, back and forth smiling, you know. I woke up feeling, well better than I can remember and now I have her voice again."

"I am glad you had such a good night. You have a lot to do today."

Marcus asks, "What will I be doing? Is this brainwashing?"

Anyman responds, "When we are babies, we are filled with curiosity, potential and desire. We express our desire by crying. We are fed, or if soiled, our diaper is cleaned or we are held. We learn to manage all of our desires in this way. Sustain life, avoid physical discomfort and seek a physical pleasure. Many of us become large, engorged babies, eating for pleasure, cowards choosing always security over discomfort and hedonists always trying to re-create through sexual excess, the thrill of being lifted up to a warm embrace. For many curiosity and potential are consumed by these narrow desires. Your corporate world has become quite scientific and successful at exploiting and exacerbating these weaknesses."

Marcus replies, "What do you mean?"

Anyman says, "Advertisers use sex to sell their products, everything from tires to rap music. You are also sold on the concept that most beautiful woman can be yours only if you work hard enough to buy the biggest house and nicest car .Sexual desire is natural, my friend. The desire to be touched and held by those you love is the beauty of having a body. It is the imbalance, the craving, the feeling of never being at peace that produces perversion."

"Yeah I know that's right. Sex sells but what about the avoiding physical discomfort and sustaining life, I mean we all want to live, right?"

Anyman responds. "You are bombarded with images of happy families at your local fast food restaurant. You desire bigger, cheaper, attractive food and you don't care about the hormones, chemicals or exploitation of workers. The image of food, the taste on your tongue and the warm feeling in your belly deadens your brain. You are searching for the joy of infancy and instead gorge yourself into obesity. Ironically, western man is killing himself in a distorted, excessive attempt to sustain live."

"And the discomfort thing?" Marcus asks.

"This is fear. The Black criminal will invade your home or marry your daughter. The terrorist will bomb you even though you live where there is nothing for miles but a Dairy Queen. The immigrants will steal your job and dwindle your resources. So you allow police to shoot innocents 70 times and to have the most prisoners in the western world. You allow accused terrorist to have no chance to prove their innocence. What if your loved ones were held indefinitely in a strange land, without charge. There is no empathy or remorse because fear and the need for security have compromised your values. Americans are a country of immigrants. Italians, Irish and Jewish immigrants escaping famine and poverty but now appear incapable of understanding the feeling a man has when he looks into the eyes of his starving children. They should ask their grandparents. Ironically, the only times that American's were truly at risk of losing it all, it was because of the greedy cravings of rich men, not poor people trying to find a better life."

As Anyman is finishing up Server enters.

"How are you, Marcus?" Server smiles and embraces Marcus. He is rigid, still a little uncomfortable with the openness of Servers affection but he returns his hug.

A second man now enters the room. He walks in, bows to Anyman and stands near Marcus. Anyman addresses Marcus.

"Marcus it is time for you to begin your Resurrection. The man who is standing next to you will be your guide. He has been specially chosen to assist you in this journey."

Marcus looks at the guide and at Server. He is a little nervous but this is something he now wants to do.

"Is there anything I should know?" Anyman responds, "Know that you are both smart and brave and that you are here for a purpose."

Marcus walks away with his guide.

Server says, "I can already see him changing."

"Yes, yes. We were fortunate to find him. Are you ready for our journey?" Anyman asks.

"Is it time already?" Server says.

"Yes. We will fortify ourselves in the Bastion of Eternal Energy."

"What is that?" Server asks.

"It is the place where we have stored the world's most powerful religious objects. We have simple cup that Jesus drank from, a branch from the Bodhi tree where Buddha sat, fabric from the tent that housed Mohammed and many other simple but powerful objects that emanate from the source they all share. When we had to flee from persecution and exploitation, we would carry jewels and gold. If thieves accosted us, they would take these trinkets and think nothing of the true treasures you will find inside this building. We will meditate and pray here until the sun comes up. Then we will travel to the land of Vampire."

Chapter 15

Days ago they traveled in luxury on Anyman's private jet. Tonight they are crammed aboard a train, shoulder to shoulder with poor European commoners. Some are hardworking wanderers, laboring for little pay. Others use scams or violence to take money from foreign travelers, the elderly and those passed out from alcohol.

As a small group of these men roam through the dimly lit train, they eye Server and Anyman who they immediately recognize as foreign. The men stop near them, they argue, and then shout. It is clear that two of the men want to rob or cheat them. As the men walk by they are met by steely glances. They move nosily through the crowd. The quiet returns, Anyman, and Server are undisturbed for hours.

The people around them are all sleeping. It is two am. The train moves along steadily. They rock back in forth in silence. Server feels a surge of cold air.

Anyman speaks, "We are very close."

"I can feel it." Server responds.

Server looks out the narrow, dirty window. He sees small homes, open fields and a deep, uncaring darkness. They pull into the tiny station and exit. As the train pulls away, they are left in silence.

"Where do we go?" Server asks.

"We walk about two miles and wait." Anyman throws his bag over his shoulder and begins to walk. They walk for about fifteen minutes and Anyman points and says, "Over there."

In the midst of darkness, Server strains to see tiny yellow lights like from a laser pointer floating through waves of fog. As they move closer, Server can see that the lights flow from a shiny, black limo with deeply tinted windows.

The limo is old and long. A door swings open. Anyman motions to Server and they step inside. Server can see the driver as they enter. He is a tall, extremely thin man with a long face and sturdy chin. No glass separates him from Server, Anyman and the man who greets them.

Come in, Come in." He says. The tone of the greeting is hearty and welcoming but his expression is flat. His skin is as white as teeth and his teeth are the color of cheese. He smells like a hospice, like deodorized death. His lips are thin, his mouth drawn, with wrinkles at the corners. His built is wiry. There is no fat, or scars. His eyes are the window to his despair. He pats Anyman's back with his long white hand.

"How are you, it has been far too long."

Anyman smiles and says, "Indeed, it has."

"This is my friend. He is here to learn the ways of the Vampire. I told him that you are the mentor he seeks."

The Vampire known as Quisling by his peers assesses Server with his large empty eyes.

"I can smell your blood. It is robust. You are a man of great virtue. Although I have overcome my lust for human blood, yours tempts me. Before we are among my kind, we must disguise your scent. Otherwise you will attract Cravers for miles."

"Cravers?" Server asks.

"Yes. It is what we are. I will explain in detail later. My friend, your blood is strong as well. Both of you rub this all over." He gives them a green ointment that is invisible when rubbed on the skin.

As he rubbed, Server asks, "Where are we going?"

"We will go where the dead live." Quisling says. "But first I will tell you the history of Vampires. It is closely tied to origin and lives of all humanity. It is not what you think."

Server says, "I did not think Vampires existed at all."

"You see their work every day and on every continent. Anyman says, "Listen closely for every word he says is true."

Server finds it hard to look at Quisling. He finds him retched in a way he has never felt, not even with the crazed, unwashed men he lived within alleys. Yet he trusted Anyman and so he would not let himself be distracted. He knew it was vital that he absorbed every word. Quisling began:

"In the early days of man before the written histories man competed with the beast for survival. Food was scarce and man had not begun to farm. Men roamed, sometimes in packs. There was no society, no morals, and no code. There was only survival.

"Many times men and women died on long sad journeys in search of food. When they perished they were eaten by their companions. As this became more common, men did not wait for death. They began to prey on others, finding them more available and less dangerous than the beasts they hunted. Some waited near the open legs of mothers until the crying baby was born so they could immediately devour it. This happened all over the world."

Server says, "So what does this have to do with Vampires?"

"Let him speak." Anyman says touching Server on the shoulder. Quisling continues.

"As I said this was happening almost everywhere. There were few places where food and game were abundant. But this practice of eating others was antithetical to human survival. Children and woman, being weaker were eaten the most and many groups of humans died off because of their inability to reproduce.

"Out of survival and necessity, humans began forbidding cannibalism but not without a fight. A third of the human race had developed a fondness for human flesh. They fought hard and well in the skirmishes that broke out all over the planet.

The non-cannibals won and by protecting and caring for each other in battle, most of mankind developed a protective instinct, a sense that by saving my brother, I protect myself. Their caring for one another led to the successful families, tribes and larger societies humans know today. Almost universally as through some collective unconscious, groups of men forbid the eating of human flesh and the drinking of human blood. Men observed in these activities were subjected to the most heinous torture as a deterrent.

Flesh eating, which, was easily observed, began to fade from the planet but drinking blood continued in secret across the globe. As a result, imbedded in the id of much of mankind is a lust for human flesh and the urge to drink human blood."

Anyman says to Server, "So you see with a third of mankind having these origins and strong primal urges, we will always have people who feel only the strong should survive. They want to create power for themselves and chaos for the rest of us. In their essence, they want to satisfy their craving. They want a world where the strong can live without rules. They want a world where no one cares and they can again devour other humans."

Server is trying to process all of this and does not know if he believes it or not.

"I still don't see how we get Vampires out of this."

Quisling continued "It is evolution. Approximately one of every thousand blood drinkers became Vampires. For many millenniums, we attacked at night and were killed if seen in daylight. Nature protected us by making sunlight fatally burn us. We stayed out of the sun and didn't get caught. Since we drank human blood our body organs adapted as did our teeth."

He points to his fangs. "Our remaining teeth are smaller than your but our fangs are large. They retract when we are not pursuing prey so our predators do not easily discover us. Our skin is pale because we function with very little blood of our own since we are always adding blood. When we are full we have the same color you do"

Server says "Genetics? What about living forever and having no soul?"

"Although God always existed inside you, he knew humans in their infancy would not have the mental or spiritual development to know him. There must be an awareness within each soul for it to function in a meaningful way. The Vampire is like man in man's infancy, we exist in such a way that there is no connection to the soul or its maker.

Server says, "First you speak of evolution, now God. Isn't that a contradiction?"

Anyman answers, "God made man through an evolutionary process. There is no contradiction. Evolution does not contradict Genesis any more than Einstein contradicts Newtown. There are truths and greater truths. If these were different circumstances you would sense that."

Server nods and Quisling speaks. "We are not immortal. Humans are souls who choose to live in flesh for brief periods in order that they may grow spiritually and experience the joy and pain of their choices in a way that formless beings cannot. Humans die and return to flesh by choice. You are continuously re-born to circumstances that promote your understanding or continue the lessons you have not learned.

"Vampires have no need for death. We make no progress. There are no lessons. Our craving excludes all things but itself. We are not connected to man or God only to our insatiable desire. We are Cravers."

Server looks puzzled and asks Anyman "What about being bit three times and the blood of a prophet? How does that come in to play?" Quisling answers instead,

"It is a survival thing. Ages ago, when we bit people to drink their blood, we had to leave quickly often times, so that we would not be discovered. Like the venom from a snake or spider can immobilize or cause decaying of its victim, our bite made the prey lose its' will. We could make the human follow us. We also found if the human had enough of our venom, he became like us. This usually happened in three bites. The blood of a prophet or an Angel in a Vampire or a human creates whatever he desires. I am hoping…"

Quisling looks at Anyman "He said you might."

Anyman says to Server. "He needs about a pint of your blood he desperately wants to be human. I am sorry for not discussing this with you but I thought I would have more time to discuss it with you." He gives Quisling a stern look.

Server looks into the dead eyes he had purposely avoided. Quisling is trembling and he can see the centuries of despair leak from his eye as a lonely red tear.

"Of course, I will help you." Server says taking his hand. The car stops abruptly. They are at the top of a hill overlooking a valley intensely dark that and surrounded by black clouds. There are no streetlights or candles. There is only moonlight that seems to be absorbed into the darkness as though into a black hole.

"Right now you cannot see your hand in front of your face. Below us, it is so dark you will doubt your existence. You will be disoriented and lose your balance and feel fear. They will smell your fear and they will come. You will not see them until you are face to face with death."

"Then how do we observe them?" Server asks.

"There is a time before light comes when Vampires return to their lairs. We are weaker, afraid and confused. When confronted at this time, Vampires will answer as though spellbound, anything asked of them. So few humans who know of this time; Vampires have made no contingency plans for this. Our time of weakness is called the Simmering. Our challenge is to remain undiscovered until that time."

Server asks, "How could we be discovered?"

Quisling responds, "We must descend to the valley below. There are humans loyal to Vampires who hide in the hills. We will attempt to avoid them but if confronted your friend Anyman will know what to do."

"How will we see?"

"The humans use concentrated beams of light when they move. It is a signature beam recognized by the Hillmen. I have lights for both of you."

The two men and the Vampire move quietly and cautiously down the hill. Creatures of the night are audible. They howl, hoot, roar and scamper. At first Server is distinctly aware of each sound, evaluating each for potential danger. Soon the sounds blend in a mesmerizing symphony.

Anyman reminds Server, "Stay alert my friend." As if he knows, that Server is reacting to his senses instead of his spirit.

Server re-focuses just in time. A man appears and blocks their path.

In his language, he asks, "What is your business here?" From the shadows, Quisling whispers a translation to Anyman. He looks at the man who is obese and breathing hard. Anyman reaches into his bag. The man raises a weapon and commands him to put the bag down. Anyman speaks as Quisling translates quickly.

Anyman says to tell him, "I have sugar for you, a bag that will last you for days, and fresh cookies and cakes. It is all for the wonderful job you do here. You must say nothing to the others so that I may surprise them. Agreed?" The man smiles and greedily takes the sweets.

They continue their journey down the hill placing each footstep in the narrow beam of light. They ignore the rustling activity of small creatures disturbed by their lights. They hear the frantic bleating of a sheep. Server raises his light. The sheep's coat is charcoal and standing behind it is a naked man whose face contorts with joy. In one hand, he holds a gun. Anyman removes an I-Pad from his bag. On the screen is a pornographic video. With no words spoken, he gives the man the pad and takes the gun. The man continues his bestial pleasure while viewing the I-Pad.

Server, Anyman and Quisling are more than halfway down the hill and it is easier to maneuver since the hill has become wider and smoother. They began to move with more confidence. Server was now leading the group and slipped on a wet rock and into a shallow pool of foul liquid. He tried to retain his footing but kept slipping. The others raced to his side. He is covered with vomit and urine. He recognizes the smell from his time in the alleys. He is soaked. He hears the whine of insane laughter. Anyman points his light toward the cackling sound. They see a man with a face that seems to be falling off his skin and blood red eyes. He staggers toward them and slurs inanely in his native tongue. Anyman reaches into his bag and gives the man heroin and bourbon. He goes back to laughing while cradling the bourbon as if it were a baby.

Server is drenched in filth and the vomit urine blend is dripping from his hair to his lips. He can taste the filth that has been accumulating for months.

Quisling says, "There is one more guard who hides in the hills. Once we pass him, there is a spring where you can wash. You must endure until then. Remember as you wash each part of your body, you must immediately put on the cream so that no Vampire smells your blood."

Server loves cleanliness. He loathes the filth but nods his head. They continue to walk.

"How do you know there is one more guard?" he asks Quisling.

"We all know. We just do not know where or when we will encounter them."

"Halt." They all stop riveted by the energy of the command. The man is tall, well dressed and wearing a tie.

"You know English." Server says. "I know three languages. I am very intelligent and I live in a new home. You look and smell horrible. I do not want to talk to you."

He looks at Anyman and says, "What is your business here?"

Anyman responds, "Certainly I will answer your question sir but first let me say you are much more professional than the other guards."

The guard responds, "Yes, I am much better. I work out all the time, I have been through many types of training and I have the certificates to prove it."

Anyman says, "Yes, it shows. The others talked poorly of you but after meeting you I can tell it is jealousy."

"You have got it exactly right. They are jealous. I have the highest rank and I am the closest to the village; A position of high honor."

Anyman says, "That's strange because the first guard told me that since he is at the top. He has the highest position. He says that he sees far more people that you do and that he is the gatekeeper. He says you see the fewest people and are the least important."

The guard is fuming. He cannot restrain himself "That is not true!" he yells.

"What is your business?" He asks again but this time he does not care about the answer. He just wants them to go so that he can confront the guard Anyman spoke of. Anyman reaches in his bag and responds.

"I have an award that I am supposed to give to the top guard. I thought it was you but now I am confused. I do not know who to give it to."

The guard says, "Wait here. I am going to straighten this out right now. What I beautiful award; I will be the award winner." He rushes up the hill.

They continue to descend to the valley. Anyman and Server follow Quisling to the stream. Server would love to linger in the water but washes quickly. As they reach the valley, darkness has begun to recede.

"It is time. Follow me." Quisling says.

Their eyes adjust as darkness relents. Layer after layer pass quickly like through an old nickelodeon machine. They begin to see the images, silhouettes, moving quickly in jerking motions. They move all around them large, bustling, and barely visible as though existing in another dimension. As each Vampire passes them, they feel chilling cold. Server is still wet and can feel the cold in his bones.

Quisling says, "Hold out your arm and try to catch one as if you are trying to catch a fish in a river."

Anyman and Server respond, grasping and missing. At first, they move quickly and haphazardly, and then become more deliberate. Server is the first to stop a Vampire who at first exposes his fangs and lurches as if about to pounce and then surrenders to Server's grasp.

Quisling says, "Ask him anything you want to know."

Server's heart is racing. "Explain your craving."

The Vampire answers stoically and is let go by Server. Repeatedly Server and Anyman catch and release Vampires smelling them, touching and questioning them. When they have had enough questions, Server looks at Quisling. He finds a sharp edged rock and cuts his hand, allowing Quisling to feed. He ends his drinking and leaps into the vortex of darkness.

Anyman says, "Sometime within the next few days he will be human. He is one of many you will save with your blood."

Chapter 16

"Yeah, I know the guy, Server. His name is Joe; I slept next to him an alley near the park." Beck Lowbrow eyes restrain tears of joy.

"So the guy liberals are treating like Jesus is really a homeless man that sleeps in the alley?"

"Yes, he is a bum like me." The man answers.

Lowbrow says, "So I know sometimes you guys are hungry and have to eat out of trash cans. Did you ever see him do that?"

"Yeah, he eats garbage sometime." Jacob, the homeless man answers.

"Have you ever heard him say anything crazy?" Lowbrow asks.

"He was always preaching. Acting like he was better than us, like he was God or something."

"What else can you tell us about him?" Lowbrow asks.

Racine and Noble were at SLD after hours watching the tape.

Noble says, "This is where Lowbrow fucks up. I can't believe he asks this guy off the street who he never met an open-ended question."

Racine says "Like the lawyers say, you never ask a question when you don't know the answer"

Jacob responds, "I can tell you that he turns orange."

Lowbrow responds confused. "You mean his skin gets like a tanned look from the sun?"

"No I mean he turns orange like a fruit whenever a bug goes by. You know the Volkswagen Beetle, you know that's Hitler's car."

The joy had left Lowbrow's happy face and he was now desperate to save his live interview.

"Thank you. You heard it folks. The liberal savior is a homeless man or like Jacob says a bum."

As he speaks, Wolf's cameraman zooms in on Lowbrow, excluding Jacob. But they haven't turned off his microphone so you can still hear him.

"Sometimes I can see his liver and there are baby unicorns chewing on it and they chew real loud"

Jacob covers his ears. Off camera, two men move in to remove him from his seat. Lowbrow talks loudly hoping to drown out Jacob's voice.

As they try to remove the man, he starts to yell, "Run, Joe, run the unicorns are getting bigger. The monkeys are fucking their horn." They cut to commercial.

Racine and Noble and several crewmembers laugh uncontrollably for about five minutes. Wolf was so eager to run the story first; they picked a psychotic as the subject for the interview and then failed to control it.

When they finish laughing Racine asks Noble to her office. She says, "You know we got lucky."

"I know, I know." He says wiping his eyes.

Racine continues, "It's just a matter of time. They were embarrassed tonight but the story is going to get out."

Noble responds, "There is more. His family history is not that great. His mother was probably a schizophrenic."

Racine nods her head. "I always suspected that there might be something wrong with our hero."

"Racine, I didn't say he was schizophrenic, I said his mother might have been." He said, feeling annoyed and desperate.

Racine grabbed his hand, holding it she said gently "Noble, it doesn't matter. They got enough. The truth whatever it may be is fading from existence. The story will engulf the truth, perception will win."

"Where is he?" Noble wonders aloud.

Cleo Bloodworthy wonders where Tiffany is. She has been acting differently ever since their return from the cave. He used to call and she would respond immediately. Now if she responds at all, it is with a vague excuse. Cleo is working on finding Vampires to bite him and increasing the patents he owns on the human body. He calls this his twin towers of immortality. The first will make his body live forever, the other gives him the money to live for a thousand lifetimes.

But he has been distracted. He is thinking about Tiffany all the time. At first, he thought she was just asserting a little independence. Harmless, he thought he would just reel her in later. But she was away more and more and their time together was less intense. Lately he felt like a john when they made love. She once had offered her soul to him as evidence of her love and trust. These days her mind always seemed to be on something else.

At first, it was irritating like an itch at the middle of his back, just beyond his fingertips. Now it felt like a toothache, not bad enough to get it pulled but so bad that no matter what he was doing, he always felt it.

So Bloodworthy decided to hire a detective but first he opened up the envelope he had on Tiffany's background. As he read it, he found that she had eminent ancestors on both sides of her family, although those on her mother's side of the family were the most prominent. In fact, her parents were the least notable of her ancestors. So he was not disappointed in her gene pool. He loved her even more.

Although he thought that her mother shooting herself was a sign of real weakness. In any event, he wanted to know more about the circumstances of her death. He asked the detective agency president to also look into her mother's death and he had just arrived.

"Sir, it is Matt Flint from Discovery."

Cleo says, "Matt come in. Let us go to my study. We can talk there." Matt follows him and takes a seat when it is offered.

Cleo asks, "What do you have for me?"

Matt is a tall man with broad shoulders. He is dressed in dark conservative colors. He wears nothing that would make him stand out in a crowd. He learned to dress this way so that he would be inconspicuous when tailing suspects. Although these days that kind of work is done by his subordinates, he retains old habits.

"Do you want me to start with Tiffany-Mercedes or the mother?"

Cleo Bloodworthy was eager to hear about Tiffany but was intrigued with the mother's death. "Her mother " He says.

Matt takes out his glasses from a case, wipes them off and begins.

"Her name was Penny Thurston. Her father was an inventor, who had two successful inventions and invested well. He doted on Penny and was generous with his time, affection and money. Her mother was the chief financial officer of a mid-sized company. She worked 60-hour weeks and by all accounts loved her work and tolerated her family. Penny was an only child."

Bloodworthy motions for Matt to skip ahead. Matt continues,

"Okay her childhood was pretty average until her father's early death. She started to harden after that. She began to act more like her mother and entered college as an accounting major. She was a loner and sometimes went alone to the movies. She had just left a movie playing in the small town near the college when she was raped. Her mother was not emotionally available for her but her roommate was. They had a long-term lesbian affair, which ended when she returned home from college.

"She went to work for her mother's company and hated it. Men found her attractive but she despised and feared most men after the rape. Richard, the man who would become her husband, was different. He was not like the Type A Personalities that approached her at the job. He was care-free and fun-loving and really seemed to enjoy being with her. She gradually trusted him and married him, partly because she was so lonely and partly to quit her mother's firm. The fragile relationship she had with her mother ended after she disobeyed her mother and married Richard.

"She and her mother did not talk to each other until Tiffany was born. For some unknown reason she liked Tiffany instantly. Penny knew that the only reason her mother tolerated her was to see her grandchild but she was permitted to see her anyway. Their relationship remained strained.

"Penny's marriage was great at first but went flat. She resumed a lesbian relationship in secret with a female version of her father. Her lesbian lover was exciting, impulsive and eventually chaotic. She slowly lost her mind and Penny could not help. It reminded her of her inability to help her father when her dad slowly died from cancer. Shortly after, she killed herself. It is not clear if Tiffany knew of the relationship."

Matt had delivered his report without feeling, maintaining a deadpan expression. It was his way of being part of the report. His reports could sometime elicit intense emotions. He did not want to embarrass them or be the messenger they wanted to kill.

Bloodworthy found the report interesting but it held nothing that he felt passionately about. He said "And Tiffany?"

"Now Mr. Bloodworthy, just to clarify, you want only present information about where she is going when not with you, no history. Correct?"

"Correct." Bloodworthy says.

"Well, excluding self-care, museum and art exhibits, library, walks in the park, that sort of thing, she does two things."

"Well?" Bloodworthy says impatiently.

"Did you know she goes to therapy?"

"For what?" Cleo asks.

"Mental health groups and individual therapy. If you want to know what she talks about I can get the notes."

"Maybe later. What's the other thing?"

She has a friend, a woman. She sees her quite often. They go a lot of places together movies, the theater, exhibits and this woman's house in the Bronx." Matt says with the deadpan.

"What are you saying? Is she fucking her?" Bloodworthy asks.

"We have not seen any evidence of that. None, just hugging, holding hands. Shit women do when they are close friends."

Bloodworthy is relieved but a little suspicious. "Then why bring it up?"

"Mr. Bloodworthy they spend a lot of time together and you know like they say the apple don't fall far from the tree."

"Anything else?" Bloodworthy asks.

"Yeah, this woman goes to therapy too. They are in the same group. The woman Shevonne also belongs to some kind of cult and Tiffany has been observed there once. The cult is run by the guy they call Server. He has been all over the news"

Bloodworthy says, "You have addresses for these places?"

"Yes" Matt replies.

Bloodworthy says, "I want you to put a regular tail on her. She has already told me she is going to be busy until late tonight. If she is with this woman-What is her name?"

"Shevonne." Matt says.

"If she is with this Shevonne, give me a call." Cleo instructs him.

"Sure." Matt says.

"Good, thank you."

Cleo shakes his hand and he leaves. Bloodworthy reads the report carefully after Matt leaves. He sees that TM is in therapy right now. He decides that he will follow her tonight.

When Tiffany and Shevonne leave therapy, they go to Central Park.

"Taste one." Shevonne says to Tiffany.

Tiffany says, "I'm not going to eat a hot dog Shevonne. Do you know what's in that stuff?"

Tiffany says, "What do you think Tiffany, that after years of eating salads and vitamins and all that pure from the sun rainbow certified food you eat, one hot dog is going to transform you." Tiffany is laughing.

Shevonne continues, "I think you scared you gonna like it and you gonna end up on the street giving blow jobs to get hot dogs."

Tiffany says, "Shevonne I can't do it." She says still laughing. "I can't get my brain to forget what's in it and that it's sitting in that dirty water all day."

"Okay" Shevonne says, "What you got in your little bag?"

"Roasted free range chicken in a wrap." Shevonne looks at her,

"How you gonna get any butt eating that?"

Tiffany gets up off the bench twirls and flips her hair and says, "Girl you know I look good."

Two guys who are passing by take in the sight. Shevonne points at them laughing, "Yeah you definitely got something. Those guys look like deer in the headlights, like they couldn't move until you sat down. Okay you proved your point."

They eat and watch people ride bikes and roller skate. Tiffany says, "You see how happy some of these people look. I used to watch people all the time after my mother died and wondered if anybody was happy."

Shevonne says, "You mean happy like all the time."

Tiffany smiles and continues, "Like in McDonalds commercials."

Shevonne says, "I think that like some people were born good athletes or smart, some people are better at being happy."

"Have you ever known anybody like that? I mean that you see a lot; someone who is really happy."

"I know a lot of people who party and dull the pain but that shit catches up with you." She thought a minute. "Cleverness, his cousin Racine I think she one of those people who is better at being happy. It look like she deflects bad things and bad people. It's like she gives off some smell or some vibe that repels the kind of shit we been through."

Tiffany took a bite of her chicken. There was a short silence and she said, "I would sure like to get some of that on me." Shevonne nodded.

Tiffany said, "I hope it's not like that though, Shevonne. I hope it is not genetic or magic. I hope it's something regular people can learn."

She looks at TM and sees that she is near tears.

"Tiffany I think you have been a lot happier lately. You are doing great in therapy and Server said he felt that you are meant to do something special. I was a little jealous. He never has said that to me."

Tiffany smiles, "I really see what you mean about him." She smiles and says, "I'm not trying to take your man. I think if anyone can give another person that magic, it is him."

"He says we all have it in us but that we are too distracted with bullshit. Well he didn't say bullshit. But he said that he has constructed the kind of life where prayer, meditation and spiritual growth are more important than circumstances."

"Is he back?"

"Yes." Shevonne says.

"He and Cleverness were together but neither one of them will talk about where they were. Oh girl, Server is not my man anymore!" Shevonne says.

"What! Tiffany says.

"Yeah Cleverness has really changed. He is now so loving and spiritual like Server but he is somebody I've known and loved for years. I've made my choice. So if you want Server it's okay."

"No I would mess him up." Tiffany says, "I am finally beginning to accept that I am   a good person but I would hurt him."

Shevonne laughs, "Probably so." It is getting dark and they start to walk.

"Let's go see him. We both need as much guidance as we can."

Tiffany says."Ain't that the truth." Shevonne exclaims in agreement. They embrace.

Terry Stiles watches them hug. He has never liked Shevonne much. He knew that she made Server uncomfortable and that she was flaky. She was unpredictable, an uncontrolled variable that could affect Server's safety.

He knew the boss did not like being protected. He made that quite clear. He also knew Server would resent him spying on Shevonne. But Terry had decided to use his organization of veterans to provide undercover support, recognizance and security for Server. He also investigated some of the people who had written threats. He felt God had given him this mission and he pursued it with religious fervor.

Sure Server had disapproved but that is what he would expect a holy man to say. God had placed him in front of the twin towers and God had inspired him to go to Iraq and Afghanistan. It did not make sense that he should have experienced all that suffering and death, if not to prepare him this mission. Otherwise, the events in his life would seem so cruel and random. No, bodyguard of the Prophet seemed more fitting so he embraced it.

It was when he was trying to find damaging info on Cleo Bloodworthy, the owner of Wolf News that he first saw Tiffany. Wolf was Server's most notable public enemy. He was seeking vulnerabilities.

He had even located a vet, who had joined the network to act as a spy. He reasoned that if they ever got any information to hurt Server, it would be good to have intel against Wolf he could threaten to counter-expose. Men like Cleo Bloodworthy never suspect that anyone would do to them what they did to others. It made him an easy target.

While reviewing the report he first saw Tiffany on the arm of Bloodworthy. As a former ladies man he could not ignore her powerful femininity. She stuck in his head. He rationalized that she was important enough to research so he asked for more information on her. He became more and more intrigued by her and decided that he wanted to see her in person. He assigned a veteran to monitor her daily activities for two weeks. He noticed that she was always alone on Thursdays at three o'clock. He waited for her to come out of the building that she entered at three o'clock and intended to follow her.

He was shocked and alarmed when he saw her and Shevonne exit together. In his mind, Shevonne was no longer just a flake; she was now a threat. Was she inadvertently feeding information to Bloodworthy through Tiffany? He decided to conduct surveillance on Shevonne and Tiffany personally. By the time Server returned home Terry was very suspicious of Shevonne and infatuated with Tiffany.

Tonight he watched them arrive at Servers office. He waited for them to go in the building and was about to enter when he saw Bloodworthy's limo arrive. He called one of his associates and arranged for him to watch the limo. When the associate arrived, he hurried upstairs.

Tiffany and Shevonne were sitting with Server. Terry came in and introduced himself to Tiffany. They all acknowledged him and Server continued speaking.

"You have all that most would desire. You have wealth or access to it and beauty that is rare and fascinating. Yet what I see in you, in your being, is incredible sadness, loneliness and guilt."

Terry had been watching Tiffany, it was hard not to. She was magnificent up close. He was amazed Server could see beyond such a remarkable surface. As Server described the sadness in her being, she seemed to get smaller, less vibrant, less compelling.

"Can you help me?" she said to Server, tears swelling in her eyes.

Server got up, took her hand and said "Come with me." He took her to the private room where he prays. He said to her "The first thing you must do is to eliminate what is evil in your life. I know you recognize evil because you are good."

"You don't know me. I'm not good." She says with her head down. "I do know you and I know you have done bad things. Your goodness is like a large muscled bearded man. This man has decided to wear a dress, earrings and heels. The things the man puts on is not the man and this is obvious to any who can see. The things you put on you are not in your nature and don't disguise who you really are.

"I am going to help you to return to your natural state. Then it is you must choose to stay who you are. If you return to those choices, which profane you, you will never feel peace. Is peace what you desire more than all other things?"

Without hesitation she cries out "Yes please, yes!"

They remain in the room for an hour. When she exits, she runs to tell Shevonne what she has experienced but she is not there. She asks Terry Stiles and he says, "She is gone. I told her who your boyfriend is and what you are trying to do. I told her that you were just using her to get to Server."

"What? What are you talking about? Where did she go?" Tiffany asks.

Server asks, "What are you talking about Terry?"

"She is the girlfriend of the head of Wolf news and she has befriended Shevonne to get to you. Her boyfriend's limousine is outside right now."

Tiffany exclaims, "Cleo's here?"

Terry gets a beep from his phone. It is a special ring. "Yes." He said. He answers the phone and his face reddens and he says, "Come up."

"What is it?" Server asked.

Terry answers, his eyes are downcast, "They took Shevonne. They threw her in the limo. I had a guy watching the limo but they spotted him tailing them and lost him. He is back now and on his way up."

Tiffany says, "We have to get her. We must save her."

Terry replies, "We should ask you where she is. Was this the plan, to kidnap her and force her to tell everything she knows?"

Tiffany turns to Server "I don't have anything to do with this, believe me but he is dangerous. We must save her."

Server says to Terry, "I wonder how you know these things. Have you been providing security for me in contradiction to my wishes?"

"I love you sir. The world needs you..."

Server interrupts "I know you love me but I asked you to honor my wishes. I pray that doing things your way has not resulted in our first casualty."

Terry starts to speak "Server I'm sorry. I will get her back."

Server says, "No I want you to be still. I want you to pray and meditate for her safe return. If you love me, you will cease thinking that you are greater than God is. You will clear your mind of all its anxiety and its urgency to act. If you love me you will provide for me the most you can give, your loving prayers from your still mind."

Terry looks as though he is bursting with emotional energy. Server continues, "If you do what I have asked, she will return to us in one hour, at 1000." Terry bows, finds a corner of the room and sits and prays.

At five after ten everyone in the room is silent. Some were beginning to doubt, others prayed harder. In walks Shevonne. She is on the cell phone and is carrying a small bag. They all rush to her and hug her.

She is startled, "I'll call you back." She barely has time to say before ending her call. Even Terry is hugging her. Server and Tiffany repeat, "I love you."

She wiggles free and asks, "What's going on?"

Terry Stiles says, "I was told that you were abducted and forced into a limousine.

Shevonne laughs, "No Tiffany's boyfriend introduced himself and said that she had mentioned how much Server had helped her. He said he wanted to hear more about him and if he liked what he heard, he was going to make a large donation. So you know I hopped right in and started talking."

Terry had a distressed look on his face. "What did you say?" he asked Shevonne.

"I told him how he saved those ladies at the bank, how people was fainting and having life-changing experiences at Riverside and St Patrick's church. I told him about the thousands of letters and e-mails, talking about how their life changed just from seeing him on tv. I also told how he removed my demons and how he had done the same thing for a dozen other people."

Tiffany asks, "What did he say?"

"He asks me if I had witnessed these things, if I had seen them for myself."

Terry asks, "Did he ask anything about Servers plans or his schedule?"

Shevonne said, "No. He was very nice."

Terry asks, "Did he ask questions about Server's past, or his temperament?"

"No, why you asking me all these questions?" Shevonne asks.

Tiffany said, "He thinks that Cleo is trying to harm Server and that I have befriended you to be Cleo's spy."

"Oh yeah, Terry told me all that but as far as I am concerned you are as real as they come. For a long time I didn't know up from down. I couldn't trust nothing I was seeing or thinking. My instincts and a loving God is what kept me alive. I trust that and I trust you." She embraces Tiffany while giving Terry a harsh stare.

The purity of Shevonne's friendship moves Tiffany. "Thank you. I have never experienced a friendship like yours, so loving, so true. It is like you know the worst of me and you love that. Everyone else loves this person I pretend to be. You are irreplaceable in my life. You have also brought me to Server, a man so close to God that he can reach through my facade and touch the God in me. I can never repay you."

Shevonne reaches into her bag and says "Then will you eat this hot dog?"

Tiffany laughs and wipes tears away. "Naaa, I still won't eat the dog, anything but that. Is he still downstairs? I think I need to end this."

Shevonne says, "Yeah, he's waiting for you. Tiffany looks at Server. "Do you think I am ready to do this? I am afraid."

Server looks at her. "Perhaps you need to be stronger in faith. Are you ready to join us?"

"Yes." Tiffany responds.

Server continues, "We will feed and nurture your spirit but we will not command your will. Like an addict, you must be ready to abandon the people, places and things that feed the energy that is destroying you. Are you ready to say no to that life and mean it?" As Tiffany takes the elevator downstairs, opens the door and enters the limo, she still does not know the answer to that question.

Bloodworthy kisses her. "So this is where you have been spending so much of your time."

"Have you been following me?" she asks.

"I was concerned. You have been very distant lately."

"So did you have me followed?"

"No of course not." he answers. "I had business in this area and I saw you with your friend and decided to wait."

"And question her?"

"Question her, no; I had interest in her as your friend. You know you usually introduce me to your friends. Also, this guy Server seems fascinating. Has he really done all the things your friend Shevonne says he has?"

Tiffany knows that he is after something. She does not know for sure if he had her followed but she knows his view on religion. Jesus should be marketed as a friend of business and of war. Server was the opposite of re-Jesus. She decided to play dumb and see what he wanted. Maybe she could help Server.

"Shevonne says she has seen all these things and I think he may be the real thing." Tiffany says.

"What do you mean?" Bloodworthy responds. He had always known Tiffany to be rational, a skeptic.

"He just has a powerful presence, almost supernatural."

"Really, Tiffany are you joking with me? You can't be serious."

"Okay, think whatever you like but you are an extraordinary man, a phenomenal man but I have never felt you or anyone else like that. You feel his presence instantly when he enters a room."

Bloodworthy's genuine interest surprises Tiffany. He moves closer to her and his eyes almost beg when he asks, "Do you think he could be a prophet?" She takes a moment to think. He grabs her wrist "Could he, could he be?"

"Yes" she yells snatching her wrist back. "Why do you care?"

He hugs her "TM I love you. I knew I could do it."

He holds her with both hands and shakes her. He is pulsing with excitement. "And you have the inside track. IMMORTALITY, Tiffany. He is the key to immortality. The man who brought the virgins, the Anyman told me. Servers blood, If I get it, I live forever!"

"You believe that. That doesn't sound rational."

"Tiffany like you said some things are supernatural. You know how well the virgin's blood worked. This man is the key. I have never been happier or wanted anything more."

Tiffany looks at him and sees that his lust has driven him to the edge of sanity. She could not possibly reason with him and he would kill her if he thought she were an obstacle to his plans.

"What do you need me to do?" she says.

"I want you to get him to a place where he is alone. Does he trust you enough for that? Maybe we can use Shevonne to help. She doesn't have to know what we are doing."

"Yes", she replies, "I will make plans immediately."

She asks, "Are you going to kill him?" He looks at her, exploring her eyes.

"No I will keep him as my own in case I need more blood later. But if the only way for me to get the blood is to kill him, believe me I will."

She had never seen him look so menacing, so naked in his evil. She wondered if she could only see him clearly now because of her recent epiphanies or if his increased lust had made him bizarre and crazed.

"Do not kill him. I will help you get him."

Hearing this Bloodworthy softens a little.

"Just think, my sweet, you and I can be together through eternity, you would be forever young and beautiful. Think about that, for men to always find you irresistible forever, to never see a wrinkle on that lovely face, to never face sickness or death. This is the dream of every woman and every man. All we have to do is drink his blood. People donate to blood banks all the time. We are taking no more than that from him for eternal life. I am not a monster sweet baby. Who would not do this TM?"

Chapter 17

Bloodworthy is getting little sleep. His craving for immortality consumes him. The other things can wait. If he does this right, he will have eternity to accomplish them. Nothing can go wrong and nothing will, he vows. As he is a great manager, he knows that success depends on composing a great team and they are with him now.

Joining him at the table in the conference room is Brady, who has defeated the pirates who imprisoned his cousin in Somali. Cleo has also employed an ex-General, one of our nation's finest tacticians as the second member of the team. His brother Bobby is the third member of the team because he was a great soldier and Bloodworthy knows can trust him.

Cleo leads the team in what he calls Operation Crossbow. Tiffany is included in the meeting because he is sure she will be an integral part of the plan. When they are sure that every aspect of the plan is solid, Bloodworthy smiles and shakes his fist with delight.

As they leave the table, each of them will begin to work on their part of the mission.

Bloodworthy grabs Tiffany around the waist and asks, "Are you clear on your part of the plan?"

"Yes" Tiffany replies, trying not to show the regret and sadness she feels.

"So can I be there when you make the call?' He asks.

She was not certain if he trusted her but now she is sure. He wants to be there for the call because he doesn't trust her. "I should be ready in about an hour. Where will you be?" she says.

"I have a conference call that should end about that time. I will be in your bedroom after the call. We can do it then." He kisses her and she manages a weak smile.

She knows that she must speak to Shevonne privately somehow. She knows it will be difficult since Cleo has not left her by herself since he declared that Server was a prophet. She is also convinced that Cleo has bugged her. She does not know where it is but she is sure the bug is very small and very powerful. He has told her of stories in the past where he has used these devices to spy on enemies of Reversal'. It surprised Tiffany that he never used these devices to spy on her when he thought she was cheating.

It was clear to her that the plan to kidnap Server would work unless she or God intervened. She had to be extremely careful. She knew that Bloodworthy hated disloyalty. The betrayal of someone as close to him as she was, would make his anger more intense. She imagined her fate if discovered would be torture, humiliation and a slow lingering death. She had an hour before she had to make the call to Shevonne. She had to think. Thank God no one could monitor her thoughts, not yet, she thought.

The first thing she decided to do was take a shower. She always found baths and showers relaxing. She reasoned that the bug was not in her body but she checked her body's openings and thoroughly checked her skin to see if there was anything implanted just under the skin's surface. She checked her scalp and when she got out of the shower, she put a cotton swab in her ear. She was satisfied that there was no bug on her body. She started to check all her clothes. He is rich enough to put bugs in everything but that seems unlikely. It was more likely that he would plant the bug while they were together for the phone call. She would be on alert.

The next thing she would do is buy a trac phone, in case he tapped her phones. She would do this when she was sure she was not being tailed. She would then arrange to see the one person she told herself she wanted to meet before she died. Since the possibility of her death had suddenly become imminent, she decided she would see her this week. She dried off and laid clothes on the bed.

Bloodworthy enters the room. "Now there is a woman I could look at for all eternity." He says, complimenting her. Tiffany wants him relaxed and not suspicious and tries to be playful,

"Wow we are not even engaged and now you want eternity. I don't know Cleo; love might start to fade after the first two hundred years."

He smiles "I tell you what, we'll do a pre-nup. If either one of us is dissatisfied after 200 years, we dissolve the relationship."

She says "Dissolve, relationship-huh, First we will be married, if I say yes. If we divorce not dissolve our marriage, I get half of everything including your future earnings, for all eternity."

"Wow sounds like I'm going to have to kill all the lawyers." He takes a seat on the bed near her clothes as she thought he would. She continues to talk with her back to him in order to make it easy for him to place the bug. He gets a call.

"TM I'll be in the conference room when you finish." When he leaves, Tiffany dons a different outfit and places the clothes on the bed into a garment bag.

"I'm ready." She says. He looks at her trying to suppress his surprise that she has changed clothes. "I liked what you had on, you changed your mind. You don't do that often."

"No I didn't change my mind, Shevonne and I had already made plans to go out tonight. The place is a little fancy and intimidating for her so I told her I would lend her a dress and accessories. Girl stuff Cleo. I want things to be as normal as possible. I don't want her to get suspicious."

Cleo thought for a minute and reasoned that he could still hear their conversation with the dress on Shevonne. It might even be better if she wore the dress after she left TM. She might talk with Server and provide an opportunity to hear more.

"Like you said, girl stuff. Let's make the call."

When Shevonne came in to the therapist office, Tiffany was already there.

Shevonne says "Hey girl good to see you.

She hugs her and Tiffany whispers "Just play along with whatever I say."

Then in a regular voice she says, "Shevonne you think you look good now. Wait until you see the dress I picked out for you. You will be the prettiest woman there, except for me, of course. You want to go in the bathroom and try it on.

"Yes, yes ooh I can't wait to see it." Shevonne says trying to improvise.

"I'll go with you. We have some time before the appointment."

They go into the bathroom and Shevonne goes in a stall to try on the dress. Pinned to the inside of the dress is a note that read "EVERYTHING I SAID ON THE PHONE CALL WAS A LIE. THE DRESS I AM GIVING YOU HAS A BUG. USE IT TO GIVE THEM FALSE INFORMATION ABOUT WERE SERVER WILL BE. THEY ARE GOING TO TRY TO KIDNAP HIM. ACT AS IF EVERYTHING IS OK AND LET TERRY KNOW SO THAT HE CAN PROTECT SERVER. SHEVONNE DON'T ACT DIFFERENTLY IF HE FINDS OUT I AM HELPING I WILL BE IN A LOT OF TROUBLE. THIS STARTED THE DAY HE TALKED TO YOU IN THE LIMO. I HAVE ALWAYS BEEN YOUR FRIEND. YOU ARE THE BEST FRIEND I HAVE. WISH US WELL.

Tiffany knew Shevonne as a loving friend who would do anything she could for her. Unfortunately, Shevonne could not control her anxiety and was beginning to de-compensate. When Shevonne came out of the stall, her voice was uneven, her heart was pounding and her expression was one of escalating terror.

"I like it, it looks good." she managed to say.

Tiffany saw her and immediately realized that she had made a mistake by entrusting such an important part of her plan to a woman who was melting like the witch in the Wizard of Oz. Thinking quickly Tiffany said "You look sick Shevonne, did you have a bad meal?"

Tiffany nods, indicating to Shevonne that she should say yes.

"Yes I feel like..."

Shevonne vomits in the stall from her anxiety about Server or Tiffany possibly being harmed. But to anyone listening, she is vomiting from tainted food.

"Oh you got vomit all over the dress. Let me take it." Tiffany says.

There is no vomit on the dress but Tiffany runs water in the sink and submerges it. She puts it in the garment bag and leaves it in the bathroom. Now she can talk to Shevonne freely.

"Look baby, I am sorry I put you through that. I will stay here. Just put that note in your bra, take a cab and give it to Terry. Do not worry. Everything is going to be fine. Have faith."

Shevonne nods and leaves. Bloodworthy had been listening until the dress hit the water. "Get a man down there." He says to Brady.

"I'm on it." Brady says. Shevonne has left in the cab.

SLD's producer is screaming at Noble, "Do you realize the position you have put this station in? The other networks are all questioning homeless guys and digging into Server's past. The only thing that is slowing them up is the botched Wolf interview. You had better get this guy in here quick. If he is going to be exposed, we damn well better be the ones to do it."

Noble responds "Look I know there are some rumors out there but we can contain this. This guy has never been a flake on the air. He is a true hero and people flock to him, he transforms them. Viewers are used to Wolf reflexively attacking anyone or anything that is not in their narrow view of the world. Their sheep will believe anything they say so what we say won't change anything."

"We are a news organization Noble. We report facts. If the facts are on their side and we knowingly conceal them then they have won. If he is a homeless man report it, if his mother was schizophrenic, report it and report it first in an exclusive interview. It is the only way for this network not to be humiliated when all of this comes out."

Mr. Wekhart, that sounds very elegant but we both know that the news is now more like a game show than a revered institution"

"What do you mean?" Wekhart asks.

"I mean to put on a good drama or sitcom you hire a staff of writers, highly paid actors, do location shots and crew to manage all that. The game show you just need a host who asks questions, a set and a new group of contestants each week. If the ratings are high, you have a low cost, very profitable show. The only two differences are that we have correspondents and experts instead of contestants and on our show and nobody wins. It is perpetual war, the left against the right. The audience tunes in to root for their team.

"Finally, inexplicably we got something different, a game-breaker, a phenomenon, a way out. People of all incomes, political affiliations, races and genders see the authenticity of this guy. He is rerouting people to the ideals that are important to them. Maybe instead of business as usual, we should take a risk and do something for the greater good, for the people, God and the American dream."

Wekhart says, "Look the only thing that will happen from what you are suggesting is that we will lose the trust of our audience and we will lose our jobs. It was a nice ride, you got to be on top again for a little but now it's time to end it. Get him in here and let's move on."

Noble heads for Racine's office. When he enters, he is sweating and he is taking shallow, short breaths. Racine stands and walks toward him concerned.

"Are you alright? Do you want me to call a doctor?" She asks.

She helps him to a seat and he leans backward with his head toward the ceiling trying to catch his breath.

He says, "It's over Racine. Like you said the truth is dead and I don't think even Jesus could revive it, certainly not our prodigy from the alley."

She rubs his shoulders. "Don't beat up on yourself. You brought us a glimpse of truth, a smidgen of hope. It is more than I expect nowadays and maybe he was here long enough to touch the right people with his message. Maybe he might even have a following after the story is done."

He was not consoled "Wekhart said that I need to get him in here. Have you heard anything about him?"

"He is back but his people are being very protective of him. I have heard that he is not announcing where he will speak. His advance people go in and he shows up. The crowds are spontaneous and enthusiastic."

Noble responds, "I know I have heard about those events. The problem is I keep calling and I don't get a response. I don't know if his people are giving him my messages or if he is not returning them."

"Did you guys have a falling out?" Racine asks

"Nothing was ever said but I think he felt I was too controlling. I will admit that at times I was more concerned about keeping him exclusive and my renewed popularity than I was about his interests and his value to others. I think he probably knew that too."

"I can still call Lenny or Shevonne they are pretty close to him. I will let you know how that goes."

"Thanks, Rae." Racine heard real gratitude and deep anxiety in his voice.

"No worries." She said.

Chapter 18

The headline reads, "Serving Death, So-called Server Linked to Terrorism- Concerns That he is Crazy and Homeless Continue."

Bloodworthy shows the headline to Brady.

"This headline is on every one of my newspapers and my anchors at Wolf have made it the lead. My commentators are hammering the message and the other networks are asking the question Is Server a terrorist?" He asks Brady, "Is your part in place?"

"Yes, sometime today three men dressed in the clothes that the Servants wear will get the job done. One of them is built like the Server and he will be wearing a mask. They will blow up an empty church and leave a note saying that the church does not teach real Christianity. The demolished church will be a conservative church. That will anger our base."

Bloodworthy says, "Yeah that's the thing about terrorism, you never know if anybody claiming responsibility is actually the person doing the deed."

Brady replies, "By the way the lookalike for Server has studied his mannerisms, his walk, everything. Anybody watching him will get all those subconscious cues that it really is him."

"Good, Server has agreed to meet privately with Tiffany at the time of the bombing, so he will not have an alibi. Our reporters will interview my political contacts and all of them will repeat the phrase, 'Any information we have would be classified.'

"This will give the impression that there is actually some negative secret info on him."

They will add, "We know that there is not too much difference between a pagan and a terrorist so he could have done it."

Bloodworthy continues, "We will let that all simmer for a couple of days before we make the grab scheduled on Friday."

Across town, Terry was intensifying security for Server. Server's resistance to protection made it nearly impossible. To convince him he needed guarding, Terry let Server see the note that Shevonne gave him with Tiffany's warning. It made no difference. Server banned any action on his behalf. He feared that it would lead to someone's harm and he didn't want that on his conscience.

So Terry acted in secret, he made discreet plans mobilizing all his resources. He had arranged for Server to stay with an activist priest in Pennsylvania. He convinced Server that he needed a vacation and to time to plan his expansion to other parts of the country. Server like most men with a sense of their destiny was reluctant to take time away from his mission. But a working vacation where he could work and plan without interruption sounded appealing and he agreed to go. Terry would make sure he was protected down there, as would the Priest. Terry would also use this time to build an invisible infrastructure of security, so that danger to Server in the future would be minimized.

Thanks to Tiffany and Shevonne, Server knew that the meeting with Tiffany was a fake and he ignored it. He took the train to Pennsylvania and was on it when the fake Servers blew up the church. Father Justice and several of his followers met Server at the train station. They advised him of the new developments on the way to the church compound. Server's first thoughts were for the safety of his followers.

Father Justice says, "The enemies of the truth are creative and relentless." Server responds "I did not think they would go this far. I am concerned for the safety of the Servants."

Father Justice reasons, "I think you are the target. They know they are powerless without you. They want you dead but it is important that you die in disgrace. They know you have equal or greater power as a Martyr."

"I know that they will kill me or make me a monster. That is why this sanctuary you have provided me is so important."

"My followers and I, consider it an honor to work for you. Please ask for anything you need without hesitation. We are all doing God's will."

Server says, "Thank you for what you do this day and for all the quiet, unselfish labor. So many poor people benefit from your fight to change the systems that impoverish poor people, here and abroad."

Father Justice says "Yes I have updated the saying Give a man a fish and you for him for a day, teach a man to fish, you feed him for life, have you heard it?"

"Yes I have." Server replies, "What is your version?"

"Teach a man that he cannot fish if the stream is polluted and corporately owned." He continued.

"The compound where we live is surrounded by natural gas companies that use this process called oil fracking. The water is contaminated. The land has become almost worthless, except to the oil companies. If we move, we lose all the value of the compound, built and paid for by poor and middle-class parishioners. If we stay we are doomed to cancer, tumors and death."

"We will make discussion of these conditions a priority." Server says.

"Bless you. This is happening in thirty states and there is no discussion of it in the news. There is only talk of how much money the jobs will bring. Corporations are the new gods. Hundreds of thousands have lost their jobs, they have decimated the gulf, no food or water seems to be safe. Yet the masses of Americans still pray to their corporate saviors. They are willing to sacrifice safety, privacy and virtue. In spite of all the things corporations callously do, they have faith. They believe if the corporations have no regulations, pay no taxes and have no boundaries, they will generate enough money to save them."

Server responds. "It is sad. American corporate interest has always sought to minimize us. They want to cut the number of workers or pay them less to increase profit. They want to move overseas and cut American workers off entirely. They don't want to pay benefits, they spend our pension when they go bankrupt. The government Pension Benefit Guarantee Corporation has hundreds of these companies. This happened even before the recession"

"The moral loss is even greater." Father Justice adds.

"We are told that helping our neighbors who have lost their home or job through no fault of their own, is socialism. Then they demonize the politicians who try to help average people. They elect people who believe that government should not help people and that business should be unrestrained."

"Yes it is madness."

"Indeed."

They arrive at the church compound and Server is even more inspired to get to work.

Bloodworthy is in his office grilling Tiffany "I know you were there. Why didn't he show up?"

Tiffany answers, "I don't know. He didn't call me. I expected him to be there."

Bloodworthy says, "We have looked into this man's habits and tendencies. He is not the type to just not show up."

Tiffany says, "I don't know. One of the Servants suspects me because of you. I think he is in charge of security. Maybe he told him not to come."

Bloodworthy stares at her for a moment and says, "I hope for your sake that all you say is true." He gives her another cold stare and walks out the room. He calls his brother,

"Bobby, have the men assigned to following Server called in yet."

"I am on the phone with them now." Bobby says. When he completes the call, he rolls his wheelchair to Bloodworthy and says,

"They say he took a train to Pennsylvania. We know the town and there is not much out there except a large church there. We think that is where he has gone. I have authorized helicopter and ground surveillance. When I have something definite I will let you know."

Bloodworthy replies, "Get everybody back here. I want to get this guy before he moves again. Let's do something covert. Ask Brady to get a few of his trusted people and we move on this as soon as possible."

Tiffany knows that someone is watching her but she has decided that she will never return to Bloodworthy. She has arrived at Shevonne's apartment in the Bronx and Shevonne is packing.

"Come in, Tiffany. Damn I'm sorry I fell apart like that, girl. I am so much better than I was but a situation like that reminds me how far I have to go." Tiffany put her finger to her mouth to hush Shevonne fearing that her apartment might be bugged.

Shevonne says, "Terry swept the apartment for bugs. He is afraid I might say something wrong when I'm talking on the phone and somebody might over hear what I said. So like I said I'm really sorry."

Tiffany says, "I know that was a lot to handle at once. If I had a choice, I would have done it differently. Why are you packing, is it that stuff on the news? Are you in danger?"

Shevonne says, "Tiffany, the way I was raised, physical danger doesn't give me no stress. When I was scared before that was because

I feared losing you or Server. I was also afraid that I might not be able to do my part to keep y'all safe."

"So why are you leaving?"

Shevonne hesitates then says, "Terry has it like a prison camp over there. You can't move, can't call, you can't do nothing unless him or them ex-soldiers of his know about it."

Tiffany says, "So you are letting him scare you off. That doesn't sound like you."

"You right about that. I'm going to be with Server. Lenny told me where he is."

"Can I go with you?" Tiffany asks.

Shevonne is surprised. "I love you but I can't tell nobody where he is. I promised and I'm got to keep my word."

Tiffany says, "I don't want you to tell me. I want to go with you. I will go wherever you go."

Shevonne says, "Do you have clothes in the car?"

"No." Tiffany says.

"I know you not leaving all those clothes you got. You showed me some of that stuff. They were one of a kind, some of them. What about those dresses from Paris and the ones the designer made just for you. I couldn't even leave these rags I got. I know you not leaving all of that."

Tiffany did not hesitate.

"That stuff doesn't mean anything to me anymore. Besides If Cleo saw me packing, I would never get to leave the house." She started to tell Shevonne that she would probably end up dead anyway but thought better of it.

She continued "Look I was followed so we shouldn't leave together. If anybody questions you just say I came to ask you why Server didn't meet me and that I tried to trick you into telling me where he was. I will find a way to drop the tail. Tell me where and when I can meet you?"

Shevonne says, "Amtrak at three o'clock."

Tiffany was successful at losing the tail and met Shevonne in time for the train. The two friends ride to Pennsylvania as though on the way to a movie. They giggle and chat without regard to the danger they face or the importance of what lies ahead.

When Server awakens, it is Friday morning. He feels refreshed and full of energy even though he has worked substantially beyond his bedtime. He eats breakfast and does morning prayers. Since they arrived at night, he takes a walk around the compound. He likes to know his surroundings. The compound is ten acres consisting of five main buildings. A large church, living quarters for men and for women, the dining hall and a large barn. Surrounding the area and running through it are two steams. There are oil wells and support structures at the northern edge of the property. There are fruit trees near the buildings and areas that were formerly gardens. There are thirty-five people who live on the grounds, not counting children. On Sunday, there are as many as two thousand people milling about or engaging in activities.

As he walks around, he stops and talks to the people he meets. Their greetings are warm and they have genuine interest in his responses. He hopes that his Servants exude the same warmth and caring when they engage others.

As he moves about, several eyes watch him. The guards assigned to him are always near him. They are dressed like the others, simply and practically. To most observers, they would not stand out but to the mercenaries at the edge of the compound the guards might as well be wearing orange beach umbrellas.

They follow their movements and take note of their reactions. They look for weaknesses in coverage like a good football coach. They are there when Shevonne and Tiffany arrive. They are aware of everything except the fact that they themselves are being watched.

They escort Server to safety while they verify the identities of Tiffany and Shevonne. When it is certain that they pose no threat, they are permitted to see Server.

Server intends to admonish Shevonne for coming there. When he sees her, she yells, "I'm here to protect you. I got your back. I brought this rope." She pulls out the rope and ties herself to him as he smiles.

Tiffany stands about ten feet away not knowing what to say, not knowing if she is even welcome.

"Shevonne stop, please. I am okay. You should not have come." Server still cannot control his smile.

"Tiffany, are you also here to protect me." Tiffany knows she does not enjoy the special affection that Server has for Shevonne so she considers her response carefully.

"I have left my old life. I am here to start my new life and I could not wait for it to begin. I am eager for your wisdom and to serve others." Server removes the ropes and embraces them both. Father Justice says, "I will arrange for them to have beds in the women's quarters and Beatrice will see that their needs are attended too."

"Thank you." Server said. "I am sure they will want to clean up and join us for dinner."

Chapter 19

The sun has set. Darkness is descending upon the quiet compound. Server has washed again and dressed for dinner. He wears a plain white robe with heavy rope across the waist and sandals. He likes the simplicity of the compound and hopes that someday he and the Servants will live simply like this. He knows that in the city he can touch multitudes of people and feel their energy. He loves that feeling. It is so welcome after being ignored for so long while he was homeless.

Here there is a different feeling. He is more easily in touch with the unifying force of nature. He is part of something great and wondrous, without effort.

Server arrives for dinner. He spots Tiffany and Shevonne and he sits near them. Everyone greets him warmly and he returns their kindness. Father Justice arrives and offers to let Server say the blessing.

"Dear God, thank you for this gathering. I am blessed to be in the presence of so many people who love you as I do. Gathered before you in praise are people who see your life, your temperament and your words as a guide to how life should be lived. Love thy neighbor, turn the other cheek, forgive, and be humble. These are the words of our lord.

"Lord we ask that you bless this bounty of simplicity. We ask that you bless the rice, the fruit and the vegetables. We ask for it to nourish our bodies to enable us, as you empower us, to do your will."

Shevonne leans over and whispers to Tiffany,

"Where's the meat?"

Tiffany responds quietly "It's a vegetarian meal."

"Are all the meals going to be like this?"

"I don't know Shevonne. They may not believe in eating meat."

Shevonne tastes the rice "Do they believe in salt?"

"Just eat, Shevonne, remember we want to be here."

They listen as Server talks.

Shevonne whispers again, "I feel bored. I guess out here in nothing, you either feel bored or restored. There don't seem to be no other way to fell about this. Why is dinner so long? We have been sitting over this little bit of bland food for two hours."

"Shevonne you told me you were enjoying the conversation. You just feel like complaining."

"I feel like having a hot dog but I guess this is how you build a spiritual life, so I'm gonna try. It will just take a while to get used to."

Tiffany says, "Anybody can be spiritual in a retreat. It is when life hits you with real problems and real emotions that it is hard. You do so well at that. You are kind and loving and you don't let insults and or idiots provoke you. You are always talking about Server and bringing people closer to God. I want to be more like you." Server has heard them talking and places his hand on Shevonne's, indicating that he agrees.

Suddenly, one of the church guards crashes through the window, landing on the floor. He is covered in blood. It is the last thing they see before the lights go out. People scream and scatter. Shevonne holds on to Server's hand.

"Everybody on the floor." Father Justice yells. Some obey, others run out of the building and mercenaries capture them. They are subdued and placed in the barn. The people who remained in the dining hall soon follow, escorted by other mercenaries.

Brady escorts Server, Father Justice, Tiffany and Shevonne to the church. All of the men are dripping wet since they have hid in the stream. Terry's men have evaded capture but are unable to rescue Server. They hide close to the church, avoiding discovery.

As the captives walk in the church door prodded by guns at their back, they see Cleo Bloodworthy, wet and menacing. He focuses his eyes on Tiffany. He pulls her to him. The others instinctively move to help her but are restrained.

"So my dear you have decided to abandon me. You trade immortality and riches for dirt in the middle of nowhere. Well dirt is what you shall have, six feet of it. But before I end you forever, I will destroy your beauty with hammers and hatchets. After you pass out from pain and fright, I will revive you with drugs, so that you do not miss any of your dismemberment." He throws her to the floor. Shevonne rubs her head. The look of insanity has returned, distorting her face. She shakes from terror and she heaves from crying.

Father Justice says, "Leave them alone. You cannot possibly be that horrible."

"I am that horrible indeed and I can arrange to do the same for you. Brady have one of your men put a bullet in his knee." The mercenary shoots him. The priest screams with pain.

Bloodworthy continues, "I know you have never felt pain like that. It is the kind of pain that tells you who you are. Now if you love God and you are not afraid I have a deal for you. I will let Miss Tiffany over there go if you agree to endure all the misery I have planned for her, beginning with a shot in the other knee. What, I can't hear you father? Keep your fucking mouth shut. If I notice you are alive, I will make you dead."

Bloodworthy turns to Server. "Looks like it's just me and you. Tiffany said she felt magic when in your presence, I feel nothing. I pray for your sake that you are a prophet or you will also die. I have convinced enough people that you are a terrorist so that your death will not be a crime. I will make this fast. I want your blood. It will make me immortal. I would kill a thousand of you for that."

As he approaches Server, he hears loud noise in the back of the church and then shooting.

Brady says, "I got it boss and motions for his men to cover the back".

"Leave these two." He says to Brady. "Hold his arms out."
The men force Servers arms out, horizontally. Bloodworthy withdraws a huge knife and cuts Server's wrist. Both women start to pray and cry. Bloodworthy sucks the blood from Server's open wound for several minutes. Server thinks he is hallucinating when he sees

Anyman and Cleverness open the door and light the water on the floor. The flaming liquid makes a path to the mercenaries and to Bloodworthy. They were all still wet, now engulfed in flames. As the burning mercenaries try to run to the front door, Anyman's soldiers shoot at them. Marcus picks up Shevonne and Tiffany amid the confusion and gets them out the door. Father Justice hobbles after them using the tops of the pews for support.

Bloodworthy continues to suck Servers blood as he burns. Terry's men race in to get Server out of Bloodworthy's grasp. He is kicked and pulled. Then it happens, Bloodworthy feels it.

"I am immortal."

It is unmistakable. He is no longer mortal. As of that very moment, his looks will never change. He will never get sick and he will never die.

"Let's go." He shouts to Brady. They head for the back door of the church and Anyman's soldiers allow them to leave. The church is burning quickly. Flames consume the wooden floors and the pews and walls are burning.

"Come sir." Terry's men yell to Server. He tries to move faster but is weak. One of the men holding Server releases him and suddenly grabs his chest. He starts to stagger and then falls. His fellow veteran realizes that he is having a heart attack. He knows that he can only drag one of them out at a time.

Server says, "Take him." And he loses consciousness. Anyman, Marcus, Tiffany and Shevonne cannot reach them or see because of the flames.

When they see one of Terry's men drag someone out they rush to them and find it is not Server. Shevonne screams, "Where is he?"

Terry's man says, "This guy saved my life in Iraq, I couldn't let him die." He starts trying to resuscitate his friend.

Shevonne starts to run in the building. Marcus grabs her. He says "No baby. We will live the life he wanted us to live. He is gone. " They watch helplessly and silently as the flames roar. They stayed until there was nothing left of the church but smoke and gray ash.

That night Cleo Bloodworthy went to the best burn hospital in the country. He was treated by a team of doctors who were given one million dollars apiece not to mention that the skin being used to restore Bloodworthy came from two just dead mercenaries. They did fantastic work. He looked at his face. He was not as handsome as before but this would do. He was rich, powerful and immortal. The operation had taken over ten hours and the sun's arrival was near. Against doctors instructions he left for home before sunrise. For the first time he was actually a Vampire and the sun could kill him. He could have wished only for immortality while drinking Server's blood but he was proud of his Vampire heritage.

That night he would travel to Paris on his private jet, find the most beautiful woman he could find, fuck her and drink her blood. He could not wait to feel the fangs. At nightfall, he got out of bed. He felt no pain. Another advantage of his new life, he thought. He telephoned his assistant

"Get the plane ready, fully stocked. I am going to Paris. Also get me the two girls I bought from Anyman. I don't need them anymore. I don't know how to find him but I will make them pay for what he did."

The assistant answered. "They are gone sir. I don't know where they are. No one has seen them since you left for Pennsylvania"

"Damn. I will make them all pay. I will find them all and make them beg for death."

Bloodworthy walked in the dark to his bathroom. He turned on the shower, took off his robe and looked in the mirror. What he saw horrified him. He roared and beat the mirror with both fists. He saw reflected, jagged glass and charred flesh. The lips that once drank Server's blood no longer covered his teeth, his cheekbones were visible and his ears were uneven pink stubs. He went back in his room, in the dark to try to figure out what went wrong.

Wolf News was reporting the fire at the church compound as another terrorist attack. They had witnesses from the compound and the train station who said Server was there. They said the mercenaries were Server's soldiers. The only one to see Bloodworthy was Father Justice and he was too scared to report his crimes.

So Wolf reported it like this: "Crazed gunmen from the Pagan, terror organization often referred to as Server's Soldiers have struck again, witnesses are reporting. These followers of a Charles Manson-like charismatic leader attacked a church and burned it while everyone was having dinner. They burned it to the ground and shot the priest. These men will stop at nothing. Remember when he was supposed to have stopped those bank robbers and saved the two women. Remember we told you that he was a probably a bank robber too. Now do you believe us? Liberals said the bullets didn't touch him, it's a miracle. The bullets didn't touch him because the other robbers were his buddies and they missed him on purpose."

This guy said we shouldn't support our troops, he said that if we don't give our taxes for welfare we are bad people. He was not the real thing and we can't be fooled again. He is on the run now. The FBI will probably announce soon that he is on their most wanted list. Keep listening. We will keep you informed and let you know if the authorities think this dangerous terrorist is anywhere near you."

Anyman and Marcus listened to the commentator from Wolf. "This is better than any con game I ever heard on the street." Marcus said.

Anyman replied, "I'm sure it is. Wolf is the propaganda arm for trillions of dollars of business. These strategies are well researched and implemented. It makes them more money than advertising."

Marcus says, "You think Bloodworthy knows yet?"

Anyman answers, "I'm sure he does. He probably attempted to get his skin replaced right away. What he forgot is that the way he looks when he becomes a Vampire is the way he will look for eternity. No matter how many skin grafts they give him he will always revert to the way he looked when he was on fire. That's how it is for vampires. If a Vampire gets cut by a knife or shot by a gut it will heal. If he was normal when he became a Vampire and then was in a fire, he wouldn't need anything. He would just heal and look normal again. Unfortunately for him, normal, his default look, is disfigured."

"What do you think will happen to him?"

"I think he will live in the shadows and feed his insanity."

"I wish we could have saved Server." Marcus lowers his head.

Anyman says, "Do not blame yourself. You had a wonderful plan that was well conceived and executed. You could not know that Terry's guy would have a heart attack. You Shevonne, Tiffany and many others will continue his work."

Maurice nods. Anyman sees that Marcus still feels guilt.

"Let me show you something."

Anyman returns with a large cloth folded and damp at the bottom.

"Take it with both hands."

"Woo what's in here? It is moving. Is it a small animal?" Marcus asks.

"Open it carefully." Marcus unfolds the cloth and is stunned.

Anyman says, "It is Server's beating heart. I went by the church the next morning after the rain. I saw it as bright as an apple covered in blood and still beating."

Marcus says, "How is this possible?"

Anyman responds, "In the telling of the human story, there are tales that cross continents. One of the tales is of the blessed heart, a heart that will endure all manner of physical pain or discomfort to advance the virtue of humanity. This heart has lived in kings, peasants, builders, philosophers and priest."

"How is the heart moved from person to person? I mean there was no open heart surgery years ago."

"No, you're right. Someone's ordinary heart would stop beating and then they would miraculously recover with a new strong heart, this heart. These mostly ordinary men go on to lead extraordinary lives after their heart attack. It is likely what happened to the man who burned in the church. He was a just a homeless man who had a heart attack and God sent him the server's heart. So do not fell sorrow for him. His life was better than it has ever been and he had the chance to make a difference."

Marcus asks, "What will you do with the heart?"

"I will take it back with me; keep it with the other holy things at the Bastion of Eternal Energy. When the time is right it will disappear, creating a new Server for the human race. The next one will have amazing influence, he will be mankind's 700th, if my assessor's calculations are correct."

"How can you know for sure?"

"I do not, that is what makes us men."

Anyman says, "Let's listen to your cousin I have come to enjoy her love of truth. It gives me hope for us all."

Tiffany is watching Racine at the studio, Shevonne has arranged for them to meet after the news.

Racine began "Today I lost a colleague and a dear friend. He could not take the pressure of the constant need for good ratings. When he lost ratings, he lost his status, his salary dropped; people he thought were friends did not return his calls. What most annoyed him most was that look he started to get where people recognized him but they don't know why. He could not live without fame. So when he got another chance he held on too tight and lost everything anyway.

"He is a good person and he will always be my friend. He was my mentor and he continues to teach me valuable lessons even at this moment of sadness. His name is Noble Cronkite. He spent his life trying to give you the information you needed to have a better life. They forced him to play too many games, use too many gimmicks. They got to him, in his core; they changed him from the outside in.

"There is so much he wanted to tell you. Did you know that a process to produce natural gas known as oil fracturing could lead to so much ether in your drinking water that it becomes flammable? Did you know that soy burgers come from soybeans that are genetically engineered, sprayed with chemicals, and then the monopoly corporation uses a chemical to bind the burgers, a chemical that comes from gasoline?

"They do this to the food of people who are aware and health conscious. Imagine what they do to the food of you people who don't care at all. You know the story of chickens born, force fed, that never see sunlight. They are pumped full of antibiotics because of the cruel and pathetic lives they live. The feed of pigs and the waste of chemical plants are poured into bays creating male fish that have eggs because of all the hormones. He wanted to tell you that."

"Americans love their children and this stuff is making kids more susceptible to disease and obesity. The stuff is cancer causing, diabetes producing and only exists because corporations are being greedy. When you combine this with the callous cost savings that led to the gulf oil disaster and the unchecked greed that led to a world-wide financial crisis and the penny pinching that led to miners losing their lives, one wonders why Noble Cronkite's brand of news didn't survive. He wanted to help viewers protect their children, keep their homes and protect their health. Why didn't viewers tune in?

"I have a theory about that. I think that when you have a society that is ultra-religious and ultra-patriotic, no one is allowed to ask questions that have significance. The politicians and religious leaders guide you away from the critical inquiry that would save you.

"So the conservative politician can get you worked up about abortion while making deals with corporations that pollute the organs of your existing children.

"Politicians can take millions of dollars in donations from banks allowing banks to inflict on you any credit card scheme they want. They support legislation that gives tax breaks to companies that send your job overseas and don't lend to small businesses.

"Corporations can deny you health care, spend your pension, cancel your unemployment and jeopardize your social security.

"You used to think that Blacks and other minorities were lazy and had dubious character. You said they were just lazy, immoral or incompetent. Why should your tax dollar pay for them? You asked.

"Now it is farmers, mineworkers, police and firefighters, your neighbors who are losing their homes and their jobs. Who is "they" in our time? Is everybody lazy and undeserving of our tax dollar? Do we have to save it all for the wars and the defense budgets and jails? Are any Americans deserving of our help? Is the good American one who does nothing for our fellow Americans and hates his government?

"Even soldiers are only appreciated when at war. When they come home, we don't want to spend taxes on them. Is our goal as a free society to require everyone to speak English, to be Christian, to have sex the way the state requires, and not have the right to decide if you want to give birth or die. Should we diminish privacy rights, imprison people indefinitely without trial, suspend Habeas Corpus and create the largest number of jails in the free world? Are we the land of the free or does that only apply to bringing guns to libraries?

"For the safety of our children, our faith and our institutions, we must question authority, love virtue and demand justice.

"The media of which I am a part must dwell on the information we need to know and stop giving the American people vaudeville shows for ratings. We must stop giving good and evil equal time. If we do not, I remind you of the line from Dante's Inferno 'The hottest place in hell is reserved for those who in times of great moral crisis do nothing.' I would also add that somewhere very near them in hell will be the media war mongers who sought deferments and safe assignments when it was their time to fight.

"Included, I hope, will be the sex police politicians who express their repression by punishing others for the acts of their secret desires. The liars in the church who lead hungry souls to embrace hate and close their hearts will also have a place close to the father of lies.

"The America I love is tolerant, intelligent, giving and brave. We will risk terrorist, immigrants and diversity for truth, justice and freedom. My God wants us to help the poor and the sick, love our neighbor and choose peace. This is how I feel. This is my God and my nation. Love it too or we give power and respectability to what should remain in the dark shadows of our mind. You decide."

END

CPSIA information can be obtained at www.ICGtesting.com
Printed in the USA
BVOW012311140212

282928BV00001B/54/P